Chasing Robins

A Novel

For my wife

Chasing Robins

A Novel

I ain't no Holden Caulfield, so spare me the comparisons.

It's always been the same dream for most of my adolescent life. I can barely see anything in front of me, or behind me. But I know there's *something* there. There's something in the shadows in my rearview that I need to get away from.

So I start running. I don't know why. I just *do*. I don't know where my legs are taking me. I don't know how long they'll work. I just know that I've got to move fast and get away from what's chasing me. I can't get caught up in its clutches. I can't be devoured by the shadows.

I look to the sky in front of me and see a hazy flock of birds hovering in the air, waiting for me to take notice. It's a round of robins. I'd read somewhere once that robins meant a search for new beginnings. New hope. New life. I reach out my hand to grab ahold of the birds but they resume flight. My feet can't keep up with the aerial movement. Their speed and precision through the air is unmatched by my shoes on the pavement. The robins disappear from sight as I trip over an uneven ridge in the ground and fall flat on my face as the overwhelming dark engulfs me.

And then I wake up.

For as long as I could remember I'd wanted to be a traveling writer. Be on the move from country to country via every mode of transportation that Life would allow: walking, car, boat, plane, train, and horse, whatever was available to me.

I'd never wanted to sit in one place. I used to fantasize as a teenager about the many places I'd love to visit. I wanted to overlook the Paris skyline from the Eiffel Tower and compose a sonnet about love in the city best known for it, or write a chapbook of landscape limericks on the Cliffs of Moher in Ireland as I gazed out at the vast, unchanging Atlantic Ocean.

Love and Life would forever be my calling, as I wouldn't need anything but the air in my lungs and a parchment of paper in my hand.

It's not hard to dream about the life you desire to have when you're younger because when your still in your adolescent frame of mind, dreams are always possibilities. Those dreams haven't yet been corrupted by each passing year. They haven't yet been forever packed down into the abyss of cement bubbling in the back of your heart where dreams are meant to wilt and die away.

If I could go back to that time I would, just so I could find those dreams I had for myself. I'd dig them out and plant them some place safe, so that they may continue to grow and grow until every branch of possibility has expanded to its full potential.

Maybe I'd be better off than I am now. Maybe I'd be somewhere I wanted to be.

I hadn't been home in nearly a year.

I spent the previous summer shacked up in the run down apartment of my freshman roommate to avoid my family altogether. We corresponded of course, but only on occasion. I told them I'd gotten a summer job near the college that required me to work every day, so the practicality of coming home for the summer was moot and pointless.

The last time I'd seen this house was Christmas my junior year. I was nowhere near eager to see it again.

It was my last Christmas break of college and already I'd felt like I'd overstayed my welcome. And I hadn't even been back for more than a day.

I had to leave as soon as possible. I just couldn't deal with all the bullshit at home anymore. I'd only spent four fucking days of my winter break in the confines of my parents' house in Belmont, and already I wanted to slit everybody's throat.

My family is an utter joke. I love them, don't get me wrong, but I think it's only the kind of love that's engraved into your heart the minute you're born. I can't stand being around them otherwise, especially during the holidays. Our whole extended family: cousins, aunts and uncles, grandparents, nieces and nephews, everybody on our fucking family tree that isn't buried 6 feet underground, spends the entire month of December at my parents house. Which was fairly easy to accommodate with my father being a lawyer and my mother a doctor. Our house was practically the size of Rhode Island. So much space, yet so little privacy.

I empathize with you Kevin McAllister. I really do.

Dinners were the size of wedding receptions, but were organized like a Thanksgiving feast and often looked like something out of a cheesy 1970s sitcom. I personally would have preferred it look like something out of a Martin Scorsese film. At 22 years old, I was still forced to sit at the kids table with all of my cousins, nieces and nephews who smelled like shit and always had their fingers jammed up their noses, who would then proceed to play this game through the entirety of dinner to see who could flick their boogers the farthest.

Even though I hated the kids' table, due to my hatred for their personalities and more specifically for the snot launching game, I'm grateful that I continue to be excluded from the head table. All they do is entice my father in to talking about a bunch of his political bullshit, or to entertain them with a ridiculous story about the big cases he's won, which at last count was two, both of which occurred over twenty fucking years ago. Or they inquire to my mom about healthcare reform, the many surgeries she's performed, or whether or not her department has came across any breakthrough cures since the previous year.

They haven't.

It's all shit talk. Complete and utter shit talk. My relatives fill my parents with so much undeserved confidence that it's sickening. They build them up like they're fucking royalty.

"I've had enough of this fucking shit, I'm going to bed," I announced to the little battalion of mutants at the kids table, who all responded in horror to my disregard of their virgin ears. I tried to slip out of the dining hall unnoticed, in the way a slut who had had an orgy with an entire frat house would as she's attempting to avoid the walk of shame and subsequent humiliation and degradation of her character the morning after her previous nights sexcapades.

I failed miserably.

"Jackson," my father bellowed from the head of the room, "come here for a sec m'boy."

Fuck me, just what I need. Oh how I love it when my dad boasts to the rest of the family that I'm going to graduate in the Spring with a law degree and become a big name politician in the future and carry on the Cain family legacy of being an overindulgent, less than deserving douche bag of an individual. He's always doing this. Boasting about my eventual career path, which was his choice, not mine. Boasting about my grades, which he has never actually seen, because I always tell him that GU only submits grades during a certain time period, which I always miss, and they simply hold them until I arrive back on campus, where I can then call my parents and inform them of my course marks.

It's not that I get bad grades. In fact, the lowest grade I've ever gotten in any class while at college was a B- during my first semester of my freshman year when I was naïve and thought I knew everything already. I've got nothing to hide. Well nothing except that I haven't taken any of the classes that my father thinks I've been taking. I'm not majoring in what he informs his cohorts that I am. I switched my major during my second semester. You see I was given a predetermined path to follow; a path that I didn't want to take to begin with. After my first semester of college I realized that there is so much more available for me. There's so much more out there. Hundreds and thousands of potential career paths, all of which were so much more interesting to me than my father's chosen path for me. I don't want to be like my father. Ever.

And so as Robert Frost once said *'two roads diverged in a wood, and I—I took the one less traveled by, and that has made all the difference.'*

I just wish Frost had written something about how to crush your parent's dreams for you.

"How were your classes this semester? Did you get to take that Criminal Adjudication class you wanted to be in?"

That *I* wanted to be in? Listen to him.

I should just stop beating around the bush and just fucking tell him that I hated anything and everything that had to do with his stupid pre-law bullshit. I should just stand on the table and announce to everyone in this damn house that I've been majoring in English with a concentration in Creative Writing for the past four years and not pre-law. I was watering the last seed buried within the depths of my heart and trying valiantly to get as much sunlight in for that dream to grow into something. Pre-law is a fucking joke. I wanted to let them know that I was no longer my father's fucking guinea pig. I wanted to see their reactions. I wanted them to choke on the words. I wanted to see if it would give my father a heart attack.

"No, it got booked up pretty quick. I couldn't get into it."

Way to go, pussy.

"Aw that's too bad. It's a beneficial course to have under your belt. Maybe next semester?"

Just tell him. Get it over with. Rip his fucking heart out of his chest and spit on it in front of every damn family member who has ever mooched off of him for finances, and never paid him back. Uncle Louie, Aunt Jo, Grandpa Jack, all of them. Cut it up into little fucking pieces and feed it to every one of these fake, money-grubbing whores.

"Yeah, I don't know about that."

"Oh? Haven't you signed up for your last semester of classes yet?"

Just do it already. Destroy the dreams he's set out for his only son. Tear that damn "Head of the Household, Decider of my Fate" rug out from under his feet. Give him an early Christmas present that will ruin his entire holiday. Or better yet, his entire life.

"Yes I have."

"And what classes are you taking?"

Shit. I didn't know any damn pre-law related courses other than the one my father had mentioned. "Um, well, you see," I started, "the thing is…"

"Hell, you've probably taken all the courses you need to graduate anyway right? You should be on to free electives and what not by now."

"Exactly."

"So what types of free electives are you taking dear?" inquired my mother, who only ever called me 'dear' in front of company so as to give the false allusion that we're actually closer than we are, "I do wish you'd take some sort of an art class. That was always *my* favorite thing to do, outside of learning pre-med."

Fucking bitch. I should have figured. She has to bring every conversation back around to her. She should just come out and say *Fuck you, let's talk about me* to the entire room, every time someone bothers to initiate a topic of discussion. She's just like my father.

Do what I did. Everybody wants me to do what he or she did. Nobody gives a shit about what I'm interested in.

Damn it Holden *quit whining like a bitch.*

"Actually I'm taking some poetry courses. Y'know studying the Romantics, Victorians, Contemporary poets. I'm even taking a couple of workshops. Standard classes for a degree in English."

Whoops. I finally let it slip.

"Poetry? That seems a bit superfluous dear. Why don't you do something more exciting for your free elective courses? Explore your creativity," my mother asserted. Clearly what I had said went right over her fat egotistical head.

"No thanks. I'll stick with poetry."

"Well, that just seems like a waste of a semester if you ask me, when you *could* be doing things that truly have *academic value.*"

"Fuck you."

Complete silence.

"Excuse me young man, what did you say?" asked my father, obviously stunned that I elected to display my displeasure of my mother's arrogance in front of the entire family at the dinner table, instead of behind closed doors.

I was about to lose it. Shit was finally going to hit the fan. "You heard me. I said fuck you. Fuck the both of you. You don't know what's best for me. You never have. You don't even know what I've been studying for the past four years. It sure as hell hasn't been fucking pre-law. I dropped that shit as a major my freshman year. It's been English and creative writing every day for my entire college career. I enjoy it; probably the only thing that I have ever enjoyed. It allows me to write shit about worthless people like all of you. Pre-law can kiss my fucking ass. And your goddamn art electives can suck my dick, mother dearest."

I probably should have felt bad after admitting all of that in front of my parents, grandparents, aunts and uncles, cousins, and nieces and nephews. A normal person would immediately start apologizing for such an outburst. But I didn't. I felt nothing. I felt as plain as a blank page in an empty book. My mother was in tears. My father was in complete shock and disbelief. I stood there, emotionless. I didn't give a shit that I had hurt their feelings. I didn't care that I had ruined their night, their holiday, or even their year. I just didn't care at all.

For the first time in the longest time, I felt like I was in control of my life.

I was no longer their puppet. I'd finally cut the strings from the puppeteer. I wasn't under their control anymore.

Nobody followed me upstairs. Nobody attempted to confront me. Nobody said anything to me for the rest of the night, which was fine by me. I didn't exist to them anymore. And they didn't exist to me.

I didn't want a damn thing to do with the assholes in the first place. I didn't ask to be born into their fucking family. I didn't ask to be a part of their lives. It was simply the *luck* of the draw. It just *happened*.

I'd rather be locked away in my room anyway than be surrounded by a bunch of fucking idiots. My room was my paradise, a glimpse of Heaven from Hell. I'd spent nearly every break from college practically hibernating in my room so as to detach myself from the reality outside my door.

No matter the magnitude of our fights, no matter the frequency of our discrepancies, these so called parents of mine always gave me my space, and I could go three or four days at a time without coming out of my room once. And they would never check on me. I could have fucking hanged myself from the rafters of my nook, or drown in a pool of my own blood on my bathroom floor, and they never would've known. They didn't care. Some parents they were.

I have often debated leaving during the night, and splattering my room with crimson paint for when they did finally manage to get worried enough to come check up on me. Give them a real pleasant surprise, by staging some sort of mock suicide scenario just to push their rotten hearts to the limit.

I would love to see the look on their faces. I would love to see their hearts permanently broken.

I can almost imagine the feeling of euphoric pride oozing out of my pores while watching them collapse on my bed at the thought of their only son *dead*. That would be pure unparalleled elation. Something I'm all too unfamiliar with.

But I won't allow myself the possibility of such satisfaction. It's too much work. I hate work. Too much planning is involved in faking your own death. I don't have that kind of time, because I don't intend to stay here for the rest of break. I'm leaving for good and never coming back.

I have a month before the start of my last semester at GU. And if I have to hitchhike my way across the country to get back to college, then so be it. At least I won't be here. I'll take my chances with anything this world has to offer, anything at all, so long as I'm far, far away from my family.

My fingers moved with incredible precision on the dial. I'd called Colton's number thousands of times over the years, but regrettably not much in the last couple. It's remarkable how an old habit never really dies.

"Hello?" came a half-asleep voice on the other end of the phone.

"Colton, get your ass up and get over here!"

"What for? Who is this?"

"It's your best friend, you jackass. Come pick me up."

"My best friend? Oh, you mean that guy that I used to hang out with all the time when I was in high school, who went away to college and turned into a fucking ghost? What was his name? Damn, it's on the tip of my tongue."

"Shut up you asshole," I retorted, "just come get me."

He chuckled, "Why, what's up?"

"I can't stand this hell-hole much longer. I've got to get out of here."

"Okay. I'll be over shortly. Don't you go disappearing on me in the mean time. I'd hate to get my hopes up of seeing my best friend, just to be greeted by a ghost."

"Fuck you."

"Love you too, bestie," he responded as he hung up.

I packed up what little belongings I brought back with me from school and paced awkwardly around my room. Colton always took forever to get over here despite only living a couple blocks away.

Every subtle noise outside piqued my interest and ultimately got my hopes up.

I swear to God if he said he's coming and doesn't show up, that'll be a huge rift in our friendship. Not that I don't necessarily deserve to be stood up like that. Hell, I've done it to him nearly every break since I began college.

I actually wouldn't blame him if he *did* do it. He's really been the only one who has actually been trying to hold this friendship together over the last four years.

In high school we were inseparable, the perfect reflection of one another. We were the life of the party. We were like Dean Martin and Jerry Lewis, Butch Cassidy and the Sundance Kid, Laurel and Hardy. I was the Statler to his Waldorf. Without the other, one was significantly broken and flawed.

I think maybe that's why Colton's had such a tough time of it while I've been away at GU. I took the Robert Frost route. I went across the country to get a degree and experience the world outside of my hometown. Colton stayed behind in our hometown to work. He took the Belmont route. The route that 90% of the graduates from Belmont High take once they've earned their diploma. They stay home, get a job, marry their high school sweetheart, start a family, and never *ever* leave.

He was never much of an academic. So instead of more books after high school he decided to stay home and work in his father's automotive shop as a mechanic. Not much of a life, but the only thing he really knew. The only thing he ever expected.

I guess I can't fault him for doing what he knows. I just wish he had the fire inside him to want more for himself. Complacency is the devil's ugly stepsister. And Belmont has been in her clutches since the beginning of time.

I was perched up on the roof just outside my windowsill when Colton pulled up in his piece of shit baby blue Rover SD1. A car that I'm pretty sure doesn't even exist anymore. Even if I hadn't been impatiently waiting, I would have known he was there. You can hear that rattling engine from ten miles away.

Colton blasted the horn, which was cute since it barely made an audible sound.

I jumped down off the slight drop from my second floor roof onto the grass below and as soon as my feet hit the ground I went into a dead sprint toward Colton at the gate. Every additional second spent here was another second I didn't want to experience. I have to get out of this place.

Once you get away from Belmont and leave it in your rearview mirror over and over again, and casually sip from the fountain of what the outside world has to offer, you want that feeling back as soon as you're away from it. Like an addict pining for his next fix, I just want to be back where the world makes sense to me, where I'm not surrounded by people I can't stand.

I want one more hit before I'm thrust out into the real world for good. One more chance to do something stupid.

"Dude, where the fuck you been?" I asked Colton as I hopped the gate.

"Sorry, I got lost," he replied.

"Lost? You live right down the road."

"Yeah, but it's been a long ass time since you asked me to come over. I wasn't exactly sure where I was going."

"Dude, shut it. I don't need one of your guilt trips right now," I barked as I threw my bag in the backseat and joined Colton up front.

He rolled his eyes and glanced back at the bag, "What's with the duffel?"

"It's my college stuff."

"I get that, but what's it doing in my car? I thought we were going for our usual rendezvous around the great city of Belmont."

"Oh, we are," I mumbled, "we're just going to go a little bit farther than we normally do."

"How *much* farther?" he interrogated.

"I don't know. Maybe Gravesfield, Applewood," I cleared my throat and spit it out quickly, "Guildford."

Colton coughed suddenly as though his brain had absorbed and simultaneously choked on the words, "*Guildford?* As in the Guildford where you attend school? That's like a thousand miles away."

"Just about."

"What do I look like a fucking taxi service? Is that what our friendship has become? I'm your little chauffeur, is that it?"

"Dude, you're overreacting."

"No, no if anything I think I'm underreacting. I've been underreacting for the last four years. Now I'm not going to say I've waited by the phone everyday hoping to get a call from you while you've been out at college doing your own thing because I haven't. I'm not that pathetic. I do have a life and I do have other friends. But tonight I thought maybe, just maybe, that it's been so long since my best friend Jackson gave me a call perhaps tonight was finally going to be about us and nothing else. I was hoping there wasn't some ulterior motive behind your calling me. Looks like I was wrong."

"Colt, listen…"

"No. I didn't want to believe that our friendship was dying, but looks like I've got all the proof I need right here."

"Colt, I'm sorry. I admit, the last four years I've been a lousy friend."

"Preach, brotha."

"And it's not that I haven't wanted to keep in touch or hang out. I was afraid."

"Dude, afraid of *what?*"

"Being sucked back into Belmont."

Colton looked at me with a mixture of confusion and interest.

I cleared my throat, "Guildford was my way out. And you were the best thing that I still had *in* Belmont. But I felt that if I hung onto that friendship as tightly as I did in high school, I'd be sucked right back into Belmont and never want to leave. So I had to loosen my grip a little bit."

Colton shifted in his seat and sighed, "I get that. Belmont is essentially the gaping vagina of the East Coast. But you could've just told me that, Jack.

You didn't have to make me wonder if our friendship was even going to last beyond this point."

"I know, and I'm sorry."

"You're just saying that because you need a way to get back to Guildford, and *I'm* your way."

"I'm not just saying that, it's the truth."

"Say it again," he blurted with a sly smile on his face.

I grimaced and mumbled through grit teeth, "I'm sorry."

"What was that? I couldn't quite get that."

"I said I'm sorry, you dick. Damn."

"Okay, okay. No need to get all hostile. Apology accepted. But you do need me to get you to Guildford though, don't you?"

"Yeah. It's like a day's trip," I started, "you think you're dad will mind you taking a day or two off?"

Colton laughed, "Dude, all I do is sit around with my thumb up my ass. He acts like I'm five years old. He doesn't even let me touch anything. I doubt if he'll even notice I'm gone."

"So it's settled then? To Guildford?"

"To Guildford, you lousy piece of shit friend."

I smiled. It was nice to have a few more moments with my best friend. Even after all we'd been through and missed out on over the last few years, it's like our friendship never missed a beat. It just picked up where we left off. Those are the kind of friendships that are made to last.

The Belmont Brothers were off on one final ride.

We stopped at the Quickie Mart on the outskirts of town before officially heading on the road for Guildford. Not quite what I had envisioned for the start of my road trip back to civilization, but I guess it's only fitting that I should be forced to spend a few more minutes near Belmont. After all, who knew when I'd ever be back?

Colton grabbed a pack of smokes and decided to waste a couple of bucks on a scratch-off lottery ticket called Fast Money.

"Dude, come on."

"Bro, hold your horses."

"The longer I stay here…" I started before Colton put up his hand to stop me.

"I know, the more likely you're going to be caught in the suction of Belmont's gaping vagina. I get it. Don't get your panties in a twist, Jack. We'll be back on the road shortly. Let a man feed his addictions first," he announced.

The cashier rolled his eyes and handed Colton his change.

"You know the odds of winning off that crap are conspicuously small, right?"

"Huh? Like your dick? And by the way," he took a cigarette out of the pack and put it between his lips as he leaned up against his car, "try not to use big ass words like that around me. Some of us didn't go to college."

Colton scratched away at his lottery ticket as he wiggled the cigarette back and forth between his lips. He stared aimlessly at the ticket for a few moments before his eyes lit up.

"Conspicuously small, huh?" he said as he pushed the ticket into my face.

I read over all of his numbers: 8, 14, 2, 25, 22, 17, 3, and 20. My eyes then glanced at the winning number: 8. The price tag under the winning number was $2,000.

Colton took the ticket into the cashier who looked genuinely shocked that he had won something. The cashier walked over to the lotto machine and scanned the ticket. His eyes immediately lit up, but he composed himself and replaced his surprise with a subtle smirk.

"Looks like you've got twenty dollars, my man. Would you like anything else?" he asked.

"Twenty bucks? Are you shitting me? I believe you need to add two more zeroes to that winning amount."

"I believe you are mistaken, sir," replied the cashier.

"I'm not mistaken at all you lowlife prick, I know what I saw on that ticket, now give me my damn money before shit turns ugly in here!" Colton bellowed.

The cashier came around from behind the counter and grabbed Colton by the collar of his shirt. I rushed in from outside to see what was going on but the cashier pulled out a gun from behind his back and pointed it at me.

"Jack, he won't give me the money."

"Shut up. You listen here you little shit," started the cashier, "I know who you are. I know your family. I know you're all worthless. And I'm glad I finally get the chance for a little *pay*back. I took my car into your deadbeat father's shop a few months ago for an oil change and let's just say he found a bunch of other things wrong with it that cost me a pretty penny."

"How is that my problem that your car's a piece of shit?"

"Because it's not. You see that Corvette out there? Not even six months old. Brand-spanking new. And you're telling me your father found issues with the brakes *and* the engine in a brand new car? Give me a fucking break kid."

"It's possible…"

"Save it. So here's what I'm going to do," he brought down the gun and released Colton's collar before walking back around the counter, "I'm going to give you a small slice of your winnings, and *I'm* going to take the rest. Because *I* deserve it, not you."

"But that's not fair," Colton said dejected.

"The sooner you get it through your head that life doesn't follow the rules of fairness, the better off you'll be. Here's a hundred bucks. Spend it wisely. Now get the fuck out of my store, both of you."

Colton unwillingly grabbed the hundred-dollar bill and pushed me out the door toward his car.

Colton peeled out of the parking lot as soon as I got the passenger's side door shut. He was a man enraged. And he had every right to be.

"Fucking asshole!" he shouted as he tossed his cigarette out the window.

"Dude, you should slow down," I said as I glanced at the speedometer quickly accelerating into the higher digits.

"No, I shouldn't. That's the problem with me Jack. I always slow down. I always give in. Nothing ever works out for me."

"That's not true," I interjected.

Colton scoffed, "Bullshit. You name me one time Jack. Give me one time where something worked out in my favor."

I tossed about a million memories around in my heading in search for just one that could take Colton out of this funk.

"See? You can't do it."

"Wendy Fuller."

He began to decelerate, and I grew relieved that the trees were no longer passing us blurred together as if they were in a Jackson Pollock painting.

"What about her?" he asked.

"You dated her and slept with her didn't you? Back when we were sophomores, I believe. She was the hottest, most popular chick in our school throughout high school."

"Yeah, but you forget," he started to accelerate again, "she also dumped me and left me high and dry at Bill and Charlie's Christmas party that year."

"But you were her first," I blurted out, "you popped her cherry before anyone else could. And isn't she a Playmate now? That makes you a legend, Colt."

He took his foot of the gas pedal and I watch as the speed rapidly decreased from triple digits back down to a normal coasting.

"That's right, I did."

"See? It's not all bad."

He flashed a quick smile and pulled out another cigarette as we approached the town of Gravesfield, "I guess out of a sea of shitty sewage, pulling out a memory like that is definitely one worth remembering."

Colton drove a couple miles on a straightaway without saying another word. When we hit the intersection at Maple and Court his eyes widened with excitement.

"What do you say? A drink or two just like old times?"

Colton pointed beyond my passenger's side window at Tully's, a bar we've frequented numerous times while underage.

"Dude, seriously? Another stop?"

"Hey, asshole, after the shit I just went through tonight, I need it. Humor me."

I nodded my head in unwilling approval. Tully's was a place I never thought I'd see again. One of the rare things I loved about the small town of Gravesfield, was it's bar scene. That's the beautiful thing about the small towns outside of Belmont, everybody knows everybody and once you show up enough, regardless of your age, you still get served. No one's going to report you to the police and try to get you or the bartender locked up. Nobody cared. These were my kind of people.

Colton and I used to hit up Tully's every weekend our senior year of high school. The bartender, Derek, was in the military with Colton's dad so we never had a problem getting drinks. He usually cut us off after a few, but we were there more for the company than the drinks.

But now, we're both of legal age. And we both would prefer to be less sober so as to forget our lingering realities.

Tully's was unusually crowded. It wasn't typically your go-to late night hangout. Especially with the city of Belmont so close with it's Main Street of taverns and pubs. Apparently four years can change a lot of things.

"Would ya look at what the cat dragged in? Are my eyes playing tricks on me or is that Jackie and Colt .45?" came a raspy voice from behind the bar.

"It's us Derek," answered Colton.

"Man, I haven't seen you's two in years. How the heck you little scumbags been?"

"Doing great, Derek," I replied.

"We'd be doing a lot better with a couple of beers and a flight of JD," came Colton's voice.

Derek looked Colton up and down for a brief moment and eventually nodded, "All right, you's got it."

We turned our backs to the bar and looked around. Everybody who's anybody was there. Mostly a slew of younger kids who graduated after us in school, but there were a select few from our grade or older crowding the other end of the bar. Tully's was crowded with your jocks, your lowlifes, your druggies, your preppy's, and more importantly your drunks. It's the old high school lunchroom, bar version.

The drunks hovered around the bar scoffing at the young meat destroying the integrity of the place. The rest of the people were scattered at tables or around the pool tables and dartboards.

"Order up. Starting a tab boys?" asked Derek.

"Keep 'em coming until we've spent all this," replied Colton as he slipped Derek the hundred-dollar bill.

"As you wish," he said, "first round is on me though, fellas."

Colton wasted no time taking three straight shots of JD. He looked at me and waited for me to do mine. One after the other I followed suit. We grabbed our beers, clanked them together in a silent salute to our friendship, and chugged every last drop before slamming our glasses on the counter.

"Derek, another round of each," bellowed Colton.

"Coming right up, boys."

I'm not sure how many times we did this. Three, four, maybe five founds of three shots apiece and a beer. Could even be more than that. I lost track after awhile.

"You guys better pace yourself, or else you'll have to be carried out of here," said a rather shrill voice from the other end of the bar.

I looked over and saw a hazy silhouette of a man around our age get off his barstool and walk toward us.

"Who's that?" I asked Colton.

"Who the fuck do you think?" he replied.

Even despite my impending drunkenness I was still sober enough to know exactly whom he was talking about. Jim Corrigan was one of our best friends in the early years of high school. Halfway through our sophomore year, Jim and Colton had a falling out and things were never the same between the three of us. I tried to stay friends with Jim for a little while, but he tried to make me choose between him and Colton all the time. I hated that. Colton was my best friend, and I was his. There's no *choosing* when it comes down to it. I'd take Colton's side if he were caught on video shooting at the President. Doesn't matter the situation, I'm in his corner regardless.

This didn't sit well with Jim and after awhile he found himself a new group of friends. And that was the end of our little trio. Probably over something stupid too, I mean, I don't even remember the rift between Colton and Jim in the first place.

"Rough night fellas?" asked Jim.

"It ain't getting any better, that's for damn sure," said Colton.

Ignoring Colton's response he put his arm around me, "What brings you two 'round these parts? Haven't seen the likes of you in here in probably four years."

"We're just passing through. Taking Jack here back to Guildford tomorrow, and thought it'd be a nice send-off to stop in here for old time's sake."

"Is that right? Heading back up to college huh? Must be nice to have the money to get out of this godforsaken place. But, not like it matters, everyone ends up right back here anyway."

I was about to speak when Colton put up his hand up to stop me.

"Yeah, well Jack here's different. He ain't coming back because there's nothing for him here. People like us are what's bound to stay here, Slim."

Jim broke his bottle on the counter and shoved the jagged end up near Colton's throat, "How many fucking times do I gotta tell you not to call me

Slim? And don't lump me in with you. At least my family's not worthless scum like yours."

Colton wasted no time in reacting and landed a right hook to the side of Jim's face knocking him flat on his ass. If it weren't for the quick reactions of some of the regulars near the bar grabbing ahold of both of them, Colton probably would've pounced on Jim and beat him into an unrecognizable pulp.

"I may not amount to much, but at least I'll amount to more than you Colt. You ain't got shit going for you. I bet you'll end up just like your Uncle Ronny and put a bullet in your brain. I can't wait to see the day," he said spitting out blood, "I can't wait to see the fucking day."

The rest of the time at the bar was a bit of a blur. Colton's hundred ran out after awhile and thanks to the fight Derek eventually cut us off entirely.

Colton grew quiet after the altercation with Jim and appeared to retreat into his own mind rather than attempting to say what was on it. I tried to encourage him to let it out, but he wasn't having it. Jim successfully pushed Colton back into his funk. A funk that even the memory of Wendy Fuller's tits couldn't possibly get him out of.

We walked out of Tully's at around 1 a.m. I was pushing "tipsy" but Colton looked as though he were barely buzzed. We didn't get very far from the front doors when we heard a familiar voice behind us.

"It's about time you guys left. I've been waiting for almost an hour out here."

Not again.

"Are you looking for a replay of what happened inside?" asked Colton turning around with clenched fists to see Jim with his arms around a couple of teenage girls I'd never seen before.

"No, no, that's not it," he started, "I was actually waiting to apologize. That was pretty low of me to say what I said, and I wanted to bury the hatchet."

"Consider it buried. Goodnight."

"Wait, wait…"

"For the love of God, Jim, what do you want now?" inquired Colton.

"I don't want the night to end, as I'm sure you don't either. I can see what I said got you down some and it probably added on to whatever else may have been bugging ya tonight seeing as how fast you were downing those drinks."

Colton hardened his stance, "Yeah, it has been a shitty night. But what can you possibly do to brighten it up?"

"Come over to my place with us. The party isn't over. All the alcohol you can drink, I promise."

Colton looked at me for a moment. I was almost out of it so I doubt my face was able to offer any kind of suggestion as to what he should do. He turned back to Jim.

"Only for a little while because we got to be hitting the road bright and early to get Jack here back to Guildford."

"Excellent. It'll only be a couple of hours. We'll be out front waiting in my truck. You can follow us to my apartment," Jim said and before I knew it he was gone.

"You okay with a quick trip over to Jim's place, Jack?"

"After what you two went through in Tully's you're actually wanting to go over to his place?" I asked, although I'm not sure if it came out quite as coherently as I heard it come out of my own lips.

"You're definitely feeling it aren't ya pal?" he asked as I shook my head, "Yeah, I figure he's offering up free booze and I'm not turning down anyone who offers up free booze tonight."

It felt like only a few minutes had passed as I sat in Colton's passenger seat gazing out at the stars while trees whipped through my line of vision. As I blocked out everything but the world outside of the car, I was overcome with a feeling of floating. I knew I wasn't *actually* floating, as I wasn't that far gone yet. But every single care inside of me was slowly being lifted off my shoulders. I've never been drunk before or even close to it, but I can imagine that this is the feeling that Colton has been desperately looking for tonight. This must be the feeling that all alcoholics search for on a nightly basis but very rarely achieve.

The car came to an abrupt halt in the parking lot of a run-down apartment complex. Colton nudged me and motioned for me to get out.

We followed Jim and the two girls up to his third floor apartment, which looked and smelled like your typical bachelor pad. Aside from the lone couch and probably a mattress in his bedroom, I doubt if Jim really had any other furniture.

"What'll it be folks?" came Jim's voice once we got in the door, "I've got Jack Daniels, Jim Beam,

Captain Morgan, Jose Cuervo. You name 'em I've probably got 'em."

"Surprise us," responded Colton.

"You got it."

Jim searched his cabinets for a few glasses. He grabbed a full bottle of Jack Daniels and began pouring straight shots into each glass. Just the sight of the alcohol made me queasy so I plopped down on the couch, next to one of the girls who was already passed out.

"Looks like it's just us then, lady and gent," Jim said, "to life."

"To friends," said Colton.

The lone conscious chick couldn't really muster up much for a toast, so she simply saluted to both and took her shot of JD.

Jim offered Colton another shot, but Colton declined, instead grabbing the bottle of Jim Beam and making his way toward the couch.

"You want any?" he asked.

"No, I'm good," I said.

Jim joined us in what I'm assuming was the living room, although there wasn't much in there to point out exactly what room it was intended to be. Other than the couch there was a beanbag chair and a boxed television set in the corner of the room. Nothing else. The teenage chick made herself comfortable on Jim's lap on the beanbag chair.

"Did you just move in?" I asked.

Colton gave me a smirk as he glared at me.

"Nope, been here for about three years," Jim said.

"*Really?*"

"Yup. I know it doesn't look like much, but she's home."

"It doesn't really look like anything," I replied.

Jim threw daggers in my direction with his eyes. Colton glanced at me with a hint of disgust. I simply shrugged my shoulders to let him know that I didn't know where it was coming from. You should never take me drinking; I'm bound to say whatever's on my mind.

"Don't pay any attention to Jack. He's had a little too much to drink."

"Yeah, sure. Don't worry about it."

After what felt like an hours worth of silence, although I'm sure it was only a few minutes, my drunken mouth couldn't stay shut much longer.

"So why'd you guys stop being friends all those years ago?" I slurred.

"You don't know why?" asked Jim.

"No, no I don't."

Colton grabbed my arm and began to twist it subtly yet furiously. Apparently I had opened a wound that had taken years to heal.

"Oh, wow. I would've figured Colt here would've told you all about it, y'know, maybe make me out to be the bad guy in it all."

Colton loosened his grip on my arm and began fidgeting with the bottle of Jim Beam in his right hand.

"I didn't have to tell him anything. He made the right choice in whose side to take in the matter," answered Colton.

"Really?" Jim inquired, "So I was the bad guy? You get all butt-hurt because Wendy Fuller dumped you for me, and I'm the bad guy?"

My jaw dropped, "That's right. She did date you the second half of sophomore year, didn't she?"

"Yeah, but there's one thing he isn't telling you, Jack. He neglects to mention that I walked in on him and Wendy getting it on in the bathroom at Bill and Charlie's Christmas party. This so-called best friend of ours at the time was hooking up with my then girlfriend behind my back."

"I don't see how that makes *me* the lone bad party in this mix. I mean, after all, *she* was cheating on you. It's a two-way street, pal."

"It makes both of you pieces of shit," Colton remarked.

"Love is a battlefield there, Colt. You lost. Don't you think it's time to let bygones be bygones? I mean it was nearly six years ago."

"No, that's unforgiveable in my opinion. I'd expect that from someone else, but not from someone who is supposed to be one of your best friends. And the worst part about it, you can't even see where you went wrong."

"But she didn't even like you man. Surely you knew that."

"No, actually I didn't."

"She felt sorry for you, Colt. Everyone did. Everyone *still does*. Even your lone remaining best friend probably feels the same. Your life is pathetic, man. Who could ever want you?" Jim asked.

This was the quietest I'd ever seen Colton in all my years of knowing him. If I weren't filled with so much alcohol I probably would've stepped in to say something to Jim on Colton's behalf, but I was still trying to wrap my head around everything he'd said. And by the time I comprehended it all, Colton was already out the door.

Jim could tell I was lagging behind in what went down. When I finally caught up I started acting like a little kid lost at the mall looking for his mother. Colton was nowhere to be found. And I was concerned.

"Colt's had himself a rough night," Jim began, "I think he said he was going to go for a quick drive to clear his head."

"But he's supposed to be my ride back to Guildford."

"I said he's coming back there, Jack. A quick drive, that's all. Man, you really can't hold your alcohol can you?"

I nodded half-heartedly as I began to slowly drift back into unconsciousness on the couch next to the passed out teenager and the empty spot where my best friend used to be. I fought the urge to pass out as hard as I could, but eventually it won and I was out for the count.

When I awoke it was still dark outside. Colton wasn't back from his little drive yet. The living room was empty and motionless. I eased my head up off the drunken girl to my left and looked up at the clock on the wall. It was four in the morning.

I got up to go to the bathroom since it had been nearly twelve hours since the last time I'd actually pissed. I made my way down Jim's pathetically bare hallway holding onto the wall and every doorframe as I walked. His bathroom thankfully wasn't that far away because as soon as my eyes made contact with the porcelain toilet my bladder let loose like Achilles storming the beach of Troy.

There's nothing quite like the feeling of pissing after a night of drinking. Every single fluid I put in my body the night before was on its way out. And it felt beautiful. Nothing could disrupt this moment.

But then I heard a scream, which startled me back into reality.

What the hell was that? I thought.

The screams were pretty muffled but they were happening in rapid succession. The sound of a headboard clanking against a wall began suddenly and rapidly got louder and louder.

I flushed and zipped myself up before easing my way back into the hallway. The screams and clanking headboard were coming from the last room on the right. I tiptoed my way down the hallway toward the room. It was the only one with any kind of light protruding out of it.

I pushed open the door slightly and peered in.

There was a small desk lamp in the corner of the room facing toward the bed. Jim was on it basically convulsing on top of the teenage girl who was on the beanbag chair with him earlier in the night. His pants were around his ankles, her panties around hers. Jim was thrusting away violently on top of this girl, muffling her screams with his hands. At first glance I thought it was just two young people having sex. But as I looked harder, I could see tears in the young girls eyes. Her hands were in fists and she was hitting him with what little energy she had.

This isn't sex, I thought, *this is rape.*

I opened the door a little more and it creaked loud enough to alert Jim. He stopped his penetrations only briefly, but kept his hands firmly over the girl's mouth.

"Oh, Jack, it's just you," he started, "you want to take a crack at her next? I'm almost through here."

After that he started in on her again even more violently than before. I was in complete disbelief over what I was seeing. How could someone do this to another person? I wanted to do something to stop it, but I had no idea how. What could I possibly do to save this poor girl?

She was screaming for help. Wailing for an ounce of mercy. But I did nothing. I just stood there watching, taking it all in.

I really wanted to stop him. I *should* have stopped him. She needed somebody's help. She needed *my* help. She pleaded for it. I could see it in the glint of the shattered innocence of her blue eyes. But I didn't do a goddamn thing. I felt trapped. I was trapped inside my skin. I was a lonely statue and nothing more.

In my mind I was running away, yelling at the top of my lungs for someone. Anyone. But on the outside my legs were motionless, my mouth sewn shut; just a useless dummy without a ventriloquist.

If only Colton were here I could get him to knock every last tooth out of Jim's perverted head. If he were walking in on this *he* would've reacted in a split second. One good quality about Colton that I wish I could say I had was his ability to *do* things. He doesn't allow himself to think about whether or not he's making the right choice...he just *reacts*. In some situations that's not always the greatest quality to have, but in one such as this it could've saved that poor girl. In moments like this I'm useless and he's somebody special. If only he were here.

I scurried away from the bedroom in a hurry and toward the door. I couldn't stay in here and continue to witness this. I felt dirty and pathetic. Even though I wasn't the one physically penetrating that high school chick, it's almost as if I were. I had to get out of there and cleanse myself with the sultry morning air.

As soon as my hands pushed the stairwell door of the apartment building open I was shocked to see Colton's Rover SD1 sitting idle in the parking lot. The engine was still barely running and I could faintly see Colton in the driver's side hunched backwards sleeping in a small cloud of smoke.

Poor bastard must've smoked like a banshee and fell asleep out here.

I walked over to the passenger's side door and opened it up. I half expected to get an overwhelming whiff of cigarette smoke or marijuana, but I was surprised to find that this particular smoke didn't produce an odor. I thought nothing of it and waited for the smoke to clear out of the car before I sat down in the seat and looked over at Colton.

"Colton buddy," I started, "it's time to get up. Sleepy time is over. We got to hit the road and leave this place behind us. I'm over this shit-hole."

I lightly smacked the right side of his face to see if that might create a reaction in him to wake him up.

Nothing.

I looked around the car to see if I could see where he'd been the few hours he was away from the apartment. There was nothing really out of the ordinary. There was a half empty pack of smokes, the bottle of Jim Beam, and a slew of other bottles of alcohol scattered in the backseat. Your common decorative items that are customary to the inside of Colton's car. Everything looked exactly the way it always did.

Everything was in order, except for a little tube sticking out of small hole in the backseat that I'd never seen before. I turned my body around on the seat to examine the tube, as it very faintly sounded like it was hissing.

I hopped out of the car and went back to look in the trunk. Colton's car, like the piece of shit that it was, didn't even have a latch for the trunk. All he ever had to do was give it a good wrap and it would unlatch.

I followed the tube from where it was pushed through the hole in the backseat through the trunk down to the muffler where it was securely fastened with duct tape.

*That's weird, why would Colton tape...*oh shit.

I rushed over to the driver's side and yanked open the door. Colton's body fell awkwardly on to the pavement. I frantically checked his pulse and got nothing. His eyes were shut and his skin was cold to the touch.

"Colt, no, Colt," I yelled, "please don't do this to me, you bastard! Wake up!"

He remained motionless on the pavement as tears began to flood my face.

"Wake up dammit! Wake the fuck up! I'm begging you!"

There was no movement. It was as if time itself stopped that very instance. Everything around me was motionless. All of my worries and cares were buried deeper inside me. They weren't important in this moment. Nothing was. There was no more going forward for me, when I knew every future moment would likely bring me back to this place. It would bring me back to this lonely place, on this cold, wet pavement with the lifeless body of my best friend in my lap.

I don't recall ever being religious. And I'm not sure if this moment even remotely pushed me over the edge to look toward God for answers. If anything, I think it hurt my potential for ever leaning on religion for any kind of spiritual guidance. If there's a God, why does he allow such a thing to happen to those he created? He created such a magnificently complex creature, and he allows them the free will to take their own lives? That's bullshit. And don't tell me that it was *just his time*, or that *God had more important things for him to do.* That's bullshit, too. It's all complete bullshit.

If this is the type of shit "fate" and the likes of God has in store me, I don't want to move from this spot. I'd rather be etched in time holding Colton's head in my lap with tears rolling down my face than face "fate" alone.

At least in this moment, I'm with my best friend. I can't bear to face the world without him.

I don't even remember getting up from that spot, but evidently I did because the next thing I knew I was walking down the side of the Interstate. It's probably for the best anyway. The death of my best friend would certainly be the type of event that would cause me to be permanently sucked back into the gaping vagina of Belmont. And once you're sucked back in, you're screwed.

I think I subconsciously got up and started walking *because* of Colton. He had said himself at the bar to Jim that there wasn't anything for me here. He was right. I had to keep going or else I would never leave. I would still be sitting next to his car stuck in that moment.

I left a voicemail on Colton's dad's answering machine at the automotive shop to tell him what had happened. I'm not sure how he'll react. I wonder if he even will.

To say that Colton and his dad had a tumultuous relationship would be a bit of an understatement. Colton's dad very rarely showed up to school functions when we went to Belmont High. There was always a seat saved for him, but it always remained an empty seat. The only time I can actually remember Colton's dad showing up to something of his was the last game of the regular season for basketball our senior year. Colton broke the school's scoring record in that game but missed the winning shot in the 4th quarter ending our chances of potentially going to the regional playoffs. Colton was mixed with emotions after that game. I remember him being elated at being the school's scoring record holder but a little crushed that the season was over. His dad beat the living piss out of him out in the parking lot as we were leaving for missing the last shot. It was a scary moment forever etched in my mind. But apparently it was the type of relationship

Colton was used to, as I don't recall him putting up much of a fight with his father.

I'm not really sure why his dad seemed to hate him so much. But I do have a theory. Colton's mother passed away shortly after she gave birth to him. I like to think that Colton's father's hatred for him was because his son took away the woman he loved. He probably couldn't stand looking into his son's eyes just to see the same eyes of his late wife's glaring back at him. I bet it killed him everyday.

And because of that he was a professional alcoholic. I don't think there was a single sober moment in my 22 years I've known him. Whenever I'd sleep over at Colton's house, his dad was usually passed out in the living room by 5 o'clock.

I guess some things you just get used to over time. My family was the rich family. Colton's was the broken one.

And yet we *both* felt like we were missing something. Maybe that's why we got along so well. One filled the other's void. I needed somebody to pull me out of the clutches of self-absorbed ignorance, and he needed someone to remind him he mattered.

God I wish I had been a better friend to him these last few years. Maybe tonight would've been avoided. Maybe I'd still be in the passenger's seat of Colton's car as the wind blows my hair back and we laugh and joke as we take one last road trip together. In another universe, just maybe, that's exactly what's happening.

I really hope so anyway.

It must've been nearly three hours of nonstop walking before a passing motorist finally decided to pity me and offer me a ride. I'm not typically a fan of the age-old art of hitchhiking, given all of the horror stories and urban legends surrounding the practice, but I've got hundreds and hundreds of miles still to go before I'm back where I belong. As the late Robert Frost once said, *"I've got miles to go before I sleep."*

The first guy to pick me up wreaked of alcohol, immediately making me uncomfortable to be in the same vehicle as him. Thankfully when we stopped at a gas station about 50 miles outside of Applewood so he could "refuel," he must've forgotten that he had a passenger and took off while I was in the bathroom.

The next generous car to come to my aide was an old couple who each had to be close to their nineties. They were probably the nicest of the lot. They also took me the farthest up at that point, amassing almost 100 miles worth of driving before they reached their final destination somewhere around Buxton. I listened to them talk about where they were from, when they first met, and how long they've been together. Y'know, your basic everyday love story from folks of the '40s and '50s. It was actually a rather enjoyable ride once you got past the overwhelming smell of formaldehyde.

Nearly 200 miles away from Belmont and still with a staggering chunk of road to go the last person to pick me up was actually someone I knew. This guy wasn't what I would call a "friend" or even an "acquaintance." But I'd seen him before around campus at Guildford, which was good enough for me. It also made my chance encounter with him all the more convenient as he was heading back to the school himself.

"Thanks for picking me up. I swear, it's been hit or miss today," I said as I extended my hand, "I'm Jackson."

"Edward," he replied.

"Nice to meet you Ed."

"No, it's Edward," he declared with a hiss as he yanked away his hand, "not Ed, not Eddie. Edward."

I stared at him absentmindedly, "Oh, my apologies, *Edward*."

"Where are ya headed?" he asked annoyed.

"Um, Guildford University."

He stared at me as if he were studying the inner nooks and crannies of my soul before finally putting the car back in drive.

"That's right, I have seen you on the grounds before. I guess that explains why your eyes lit up when you opened the door. You had me worried for a second."

"Yeah, sorry about that," I said clearing my throat, "it was just a bit of relief to see someone vaguely familiar picking me up. I'm assuming your heading back there?"

"Your assumption would be correct," he started, "but if I may ask…why in the world are you *hitchhiking* back to school? Don't you have a family member or a friend who could drive you? It's a sketchy world out there filled with crazy people, pal."

"Well, my family is the main reason I'm leaving, and let's just say, there's a bit of an unintended void in the friend department at the moment."

Edward nodded in a manner that indicated a lack of caring about my response. I'm sure he was simply adhering to the normal chitchat accustomed to every hitchhiker/driver interaction of the last 50 years or so. At least that's what I've seen in many horrible Lifetime TV movies anyway. Either the hitchhiker is the psychopath reminding the driver of the dangers of picking up hitchhikers, or the driver is the psychopath reminding the hitchhiker of the dangers of hitchhiking.

I guess this makes Edward the potential psychopath. Hopefully he decides to leave my limbs intact.

"Hey, you hungry by any chance?" he asked, "I haven't had anything to eat yet this morning and I could use a pick-me-up before continuing the long haul back out to Guildford."

It seemed like everyone who picked me up wanted to stop every hundred feet, but my stomach quietly reminded me that I hadn't had anything to eat since dinner at my parents' house so I gave in.

"Yeah, I could go for a bite to eat."

Mary's Diner was a very small, quiet little place in a severely unpopulated area called Framingham, just about 500 miles southwest of Belmont. Like any diner, it was occupied mostly with older folks drinking their morning coffees and reading their newspapers; keeping consistency within their daily routines.

Edward and I took a seat in a booth near the front door. A young waitress noticed us sit down and began rustling together a couple of menus and silverware before heading in our direction.

"Good morning gentleman, my name is Darlene and I'll be taking care of you today. Can I start you fellas off with something to drink? Maybe a coffee or some OJ?" she asked with a pleasant smile.

"I'll have a water," Edward responded.

She glanced over at me, "And for you sir?"

"Orange juice for me."

"Excellent," she smiled, "I'll get that for you and give you two a minute to look over the menu. Best breakfast menu this side of the state."

I watched her as she walked away. She was unbelievably beautiful. She almost looked out of place in this diner, like she should be modeling somewhere. I was transfixed with the way her gorgeous brown hair parted to one side, and her ruby red lips pursed as she poured us our drinks.

She glanced over in our direction as I quickly fumbled to divert my gaze back toward the menu. It looked as if she'd giggled to herself at my clumsiness and unusually pathetic excuse for staring without the presence of mind of doing it sneakily.

"Your drinks gentleman," she said as she placed them on the countertop in front of us, "do we know what we'd like to eat this morning?"

It may come off as a little dirty, and forgive me if you don't like this sort of thing, but fuck it sex is apart of life and my only thought as she asked that question was my overwhelming desire to eat *her*.

Apparently in all that time I was thinking about tearing her work clothes off and making love to this woman right on the table, Edward had already ordered and was growing irritated at my daydreaming.

"Yo, Earth to Jackson," he shouted.

"Um, what? Did you say something?" I asked.

"Yeah, this lady here has been waiting on your order for a good 30 seconds. And I'd like to eat and get back on the road, if you don't mind."

"I'm sorry," I said as I looked up at her beautiful brown eyes, "I'm a little out of it today. I'll just have some pancakes."

She smiled again at my pathetic awkwardness and walked away.

It took no time for our food to come out. That's what I like about little mom-and-pop shop diners, you get your food right away and it's always amazing.

I wish I could tell you exactly how amazing the food was, but quite frankly I don't remember a single bite of it. The whole entire time I had my food my eyes were locked across the diner on our waitress Darlene. I tried to hide it the best I could, but there was just no use in fighting it. Our eyes met a couple of times, which caused me to spill my drink the first time and drop food down my shirt the second time. Both times she noticed and laughed, and in a few moments was there to offer a rescue napkin.

I was in a complete trance with this woman. Every move she made I was mesmerized. I was completely overwhelmed by her beauty. If I had any idea what love was, I may even come so close to admit that I'd fallen head over heels in love with this woman after only 20 minutes of her being in my life.

I just wish Edward wasn't in such a hurry to leave. It would've been nice to awkwardly say goodbye to Darlene, since it was highly likely I'd never get to see her beautiful face again.

T he road is a tiresome place. Now Guildford is nowhere near as far away as say NYC is to LA, but it's certainly far enough. Especially for someone who just wants to get back to the only place in the world that makes any kind of sense.

I just want to be back in my dorm room away from it all, away from reality. I just want to bury my head into whatever books I happen to have lying around. Hemingway, Kafka, maybe even some Salinger. I just want to get lost in someone else's reality. I want to forget about everything that's lingering outside the pages of these books and focus only on the words that blur together so perfectly to create the ideal escape. An ideal escape that I so desperately need these days.

The majority of the trip saw very little interaction between Edward and me. I don't know what it was with him, but he didn't really seem like he was interested in casual conversation. There were a couple of times I tried to initiate some kind of communication, but he either shrugged it off or replied with one word responses to basically stop it from manifesting altogether. If only he would've had the radio on at least. Then maybe I wouldn't have been forced to stare ahead of me in complete silence listening to the wind pass by my passenger's side window for seven hours.

Seven fucking hours of nothing but silence. If only I had a notebook to write in. *Oh, shit,* I thought, *I do have one in my duffel.*

I reached into the back seat for my duffel bag. My hand was met with nothing but emptiness. I started to panic and turned around to look. My duffel bag was missing. I slouched down in the seat and slammed my hands into my face over my eyes.

Edward looked over at me, "What's the matter with you?"

"My duffel bag with all of my stuff in it is missing," I responded as I retreated back in my mind attempting to recall every location I remember having it.

"You had it at the diner," came Edward's boring voice.

He was right. I *did* have it at the diner. The only problem was, I wasn't quite myself at the diner having been awestruck by our waitress' beauty. I can't even recall a single thing I ate there, let alone what I brought in with me.

I sank even lower into my seat after finally accepting my absentmindedness, "I fucking left it in the booth."

"That sucks."

"We have to go back and get it. My whole life is in that bag," I said.

Edward chuckled slyly, "That's rich, Jackson. We're not going back."

"And why the fuck not?"

"Because I'm a nearly broke college student who just drove over 600 miles today, and can't afford to drive back to the diner and then back here again. And in case you haven't noticed any of the signs lately, we're almost back at school."

I lifted myself up and looked out the window. I saw a green sign that read "Guildford University – 2 miles" that confirmed what Edward had said.

"Fuck," I shouted.

"I'm sorry, pal. I wish I could help you out with all that, but unfortunately that's beyond my capabilities. Maybe it'll turn up. Did you have anything in the bag that had your name or an address on it?" he asked.

I thought about it for a second, "Yeah, my notebook has my name in it and a GU sticker. You know those gay little stickers they hand out at Orientation freshman year?"

"Well there you go. Maybe someone at the diner picked it up and will return it to you," he said unconvincingly, "you live in Branson Hall right?"

I nodded as the car eased to a stop.

"Hey, thanks for the lift, Edward. I really do appreciate your hospitality."

He offered a lazy grunt as I stepped out of the car and shut the door. Before I could even take in any of my surroundings Edward sped off toward his dorms.

I stood on the sidewalk and gazed errantly in front of me at Branson Hall when the vibration of my phone startled me back into consciousness. I didn't recognize the number but decided to answer it anyway.

"Hello?"

There was a muffled silence for a moment and then a voice replied through soft sniffles and obvious sobbing, "Uh, hey, Jack?"

"Derek?" I asked.

"Yeah, bud, it's me. Um, this is," he sighed loudly, "this is gonna be hard for me to say. And probably gonna be even harder for you to hear. You should probably sit down, if you're not already."

I already knew what he was calling for, but played along, "What is it?"

"Your pal Colton, he was found dead early this morning of an apparent suicide."

I was silent for a minute, before breaking down in a pool of tears. At first it was meant to be playing the part since I already knew, but after the first tear cascaded along the terrain of my cheeks, it was full-out water works. My best friend was gone. Although I knew no amount of tears could possibly bring him back, the sheer realization of his absence was still just too much to take.

"It gets worse, Jack."

My eyes opened wide with shock. *It gets worse?* Did he know something more that I didn't know? What could possibly be worse than my best friend committing suicide?

"What do you mean?" I asked him.

Derek cleared his throat, "John, I mean, Colton's dad…somebody must've told him about what had happened to his son. It really must've messed him up because…well, he was found in his office at work a couple of hours ago, and he, uh…had a gunshot wound in his head."

Derek started to lose what little composure he had mustered up to utter those words and hung up on me.

I was in complete disbelief. It was as if an emotional snowplow had pummeled through the ten feet of snow and ice surrounding me at this very moment. I fell down to my knees onto the icy pavement.

I was overcome with a mix of emotions. So many feelings were flooding into my heart and hitting me all at once. Happiness, sadness, helplessness, loneliness, relief, anxiety; every emotion I could possibly think of was bouncing around inside of me. Originally I thought the only emotion I'd experience at this moment—being mere steps away from my dorm—would be an overwhelming sense of joy. But all I could think about was everything else, Colton, his father, Jim and the high school girl, the waitress, my duffel bag.

Even though I'd finally made it to where I wanted to be, life suddenly sucked. And life doesn't just suck in snippets. Life tends to suck all at once.

The Spring semester wasn't much different than any other semester in my four years at GU. It definitely flew by a lot quicker than I anticipated it would however. And I still didn't have my duffel bag.

It's tough going through each and every day when you know that a piece of you is missing. It's even tougher when there are multiple pieces missing.

The first piece was Colton. His body was found later that same morning that I'd set out on the road hitchhiking. I hadn't heard about anything else concerning him since that day. He'd gotten a small segment on the news and that was it. Nothing else. There was no funeral, no talk about suicide prevention, no formal recognition for his young life and minimal accomplishments, nothing.

It's a real shame that we don't care more about one another.

I was also missing a small romantic piece of my soul. The waitress at Mary's Diner crossed my mind almost everyday. Which is weird because I knew nothing about her other than she was a waitress and unbelievably beautiful. That's it. I'm not the type of person to fall in love easily. I'm not even 100% sure that I even believe in the concept of love to begin with. But this woman found a way to occupy the little crevasses within my shriveled up heart.

And then there was my duffel bag. The duffel bag itself wasn't really that important, but the contents inside the duffel bag are where my life is. There's some clothing and a few books, which are replaceable, but my notebooks are not. Each of my notebooks has easily three or four hundred poems in them. My literary future rests in the pages of those notebooks. I could've and probably should've kept copies of my poems on my laptop or on a jump drive, but instead I elected to stick with tradition much in the way that my literary heroes always had by writing my art down on paper. And only paper. Looking back on it now, probably a dumb move.

It was about a week until graduation. Classes were complete and finals were basically over. There was nothing left to do but wait for grades to be in. Final grades were just white noise at this point as I was certain that I was getting at least a B+ or higher in all of my classes and that I was a guarantee to be walking across the stage.

The highlight at the culmination of every year is the massive party that's thrown at one of the fraternity houses on Drinker Street a few blocks from the school.

I'm not sure which fraternity it was, as fraternities weren't my thing. I'd go to the parties every weekend and the big ones at the end of every year because it was the "normal" thing to do. If you didn't go to the parties, you were a *nobody*. And all college is, is a bunch of people trying to be *somebody*.

This party always drew huge crowds. Oftentimes there were more people at the party from different schools than there were people from GU.

I didn't expect to be there very long, or really even enjoy myself much as most of my best friends while at GU graduated last year. They were all out in the real world already and I couldn't wait to get out there and join them. Now don't get me wrong, I love GU. The best four years of my life were spent on this campus and in this city. I wouldn't change a single aspect about my time spent here. I just want to be out of here so that I can get back with the friends I made that I haven't seen in a year. That's all.

The frat houses at GU were almost identical to the stereotypical ones you see in the movies. Old buildings with hundreds of year's worth of traditions filled with lots of premarital and unprotected sex and all the booze you can drink.

I was welcomed with a red Solo cup of Bud light and made my way out to the backyard pool area. I sat down on a lawn chair and sipped at my drink just watching the drunken shenanigans of all the underclassmen. It was apparent that a lot of these kids couldn't handle their alcohol, or started much earlier in the day because people were falling all over the place and puking wherever was convenient.

If I could take one picture to best encapsulate the college experience, I would take one of the guy on the other side of the pool hugging an empty keg, passed out with underwear on his head and dicks drawn in Sharpie all over his pale white body.

"Excuse me," came an angelic voice from behind me as a soft hand graced my shoulder, "Carter is it?"

I turned around to see who it was and I almost fainted in complete shock. It was the girl from the diner.

"Do you remember me?" she asked, "I'm Darlene from Mary's Diner."

It was as if I'd never formulated an intelligible thought before in my life. I fumbled for the right words, "I, um—uh, I, uh yeah. I mean, yes, yes I do."

"Do you go to school here?"

"I do. I graduate next week. Then it's off to the real world," I said wincing at every uttered word. I sounded like a complete douchebag.

She smiled, "That's awesome. I have a friend that goes here and she asked me to come out tonight. Apparently this is some amazing party that happens every year."

"Yeah, it's lost some of its luster lately, but it's the best we've got."

"I can see that. It looks like we've missed the best part of it. All I've seen since I got here is a lot of half naked boys passed out in their own vomit."

I chuckled, "Yeah, you've basically described the school logo."

Darlene laughed, almost spitting out her drink.

"You're so funny, Carter."

"My name's actually Jackson," I informed her.

Her face turned a bright red, "Oh my, I'm so sorry. I thought it was Carter. I have your duffel bag that you left at the diner and forgive me for being nosey but I looked in it and saw your notebooks.

They all have the name Carter written on them so I just assumed that was your name."

My eyes lit up at the confirmation of Darlene having my bag. All the worry I'd let engulf my body over the last few months at the whereabouts of my duffel bag and notebooks was completely washed away.

I composed myself, "Yeah, that's my pen name. I'm a little self-conscious about my poetry so I made up a pseudonym in case I ever try to get my work published."

"Well, I don't think you have anything to be self-conscious about. You have a way with words that's unmatched. Your poetry is absolutely beautiful," she said.

"You read my poetry?"

She stumbled, "Oh no, I hope you don't mind. I only read a few poems."

"It's fine," I replied, "you're the first person whose ever read any of them before."

"You've never let *anyone* read them? Why not? You truly have a gift, Jackson."

"I guess I'm a little terrified of rejection. I mean, what if they don't like them? What if they tell me I'm awful and wasting my time? What if I don't amount to what I've always dreamed of?"

She grabbed my hand and looked me square in the eyes, "Then they're passing on someone special."

I smiled, "You're just saying that."

"No, I'm serious," she started, "will you read me some more of your poetry?"

"I don't know."

"Oh, please, please, please?" she said as she squeezed my hand harder.

"Fine, but not here."

A smile instantly sprouted across Darlene's face and she let go of my hand and hugged me. For a very petite young woman, she was exceptionally strong.

It's been a really long time since I've had a girl in my dorm room. In fact, it's been so long that I can't even recall the last member of the opposite sex who had the pleasure of seeing how a male college senior lives. If I had known a girl would have been coming back to my room, I probably would've cleaned it up some.

"Aw, you didn't need to tidy up for me?" she said as we walked through the door.

I laughed pushing aside a pile of clothes on my bed so that we could sit down, "Yeah, sorry. Wasn't actually expecting company any time soon."

"It's okay," she said as she placed my duffel bag down between us.

"Oh man, is that a sight for sore eyes."

"I can imagine. The last few months must've been torture for you."

"You have no idea."

I ripped open the duffel bag and clawed through all of my stuff. I pulled out shirts and clothes I hadn't seen since Christmas. The Holy Grail was underneath it all. I pulled out the first notebook, a green composition book with the initials C.C. etched across the top. I fiddled through the pages and basked in the illustrious scent of the paper. I couldn't hide the smile that crept along my face.

"I can see that you're definitely happy now!" Darlene interjected.

"Again, you have *no* idea. It was like I'd lost my children and am finally reunited with them."

"Well, I'm glad that I could have a small part in reuniting you with your kids," she said chuckling as her hand grazed my left leg.

I nervously laughed and pulled out the rest of the notebooks from the duffel bag and spread them out along the bed.

"I'd never thought I'd see them again."

She picked up one of my notebooks and glanced through the pages, "Will you read me one?"

My heart was beating practically out of my chest, "I don't know. I don't really like reading my stuff out loud."

"Please?" she asked as her hand made her way back up my leg, "It would make me really happy to hear your work *from you*."

She squeezed my leg and I caved, "Fine. I guess it couldn't hurt if I read one of them to you."

Her eyes lit up.

I turned each page ferociously searching for my something worth reading to her. There were very few poems I felt somewhat comfortable reading out loud. My poetry certainly doesn't do the likes of Shakespeare or Whitman justice, but it's what I love to do, and when a beautiful woman wants to hear your poetry, you muster up the courage to read it to her. No matter how terrible it might be.

I found the poem I had been looking for, "Okay, this is a poem I wrote during my freshman year, so please go easy on me."

She smiled.

"It's called *Mile Markers*."

"Oh, I like the title. Kind of a traveling type poem?"

"In a way," I said. I then let out a huge uneasy breath and started to read:

> *So she said, "Let's drive."*
>
> *Drive some place where our problems*
> *can't find us, where our grievances*
> *and troubles and stresses and daily*
> *misfortunes*
> *can't sneak up from behind and drag us to*
> *the dirt.*
>
> *Drive somewhere*—anywhere *that the*
> *hurdles of Life don't exist.*
>
> *But could we find such a place?*
>
> *Where could the worn out treads of these*
> *tires*
> *possibly take us as an escape?*
> *A hundred years ago it was probably*
> *feasible.*
> *Today, a life of relative obscurity*
> *is damn near impossible.*
>
> *So she said, "Let's drive anyway."*
> *Maybe we'll find* somewhere *on the road*
> *to anywhere.*
>
> *Let's drive until all our cares melt away*
> *as hastily*
> *as an ice cream cone on a humid*

Summer's night. Let's drive until all our
worries

are just tiny specks of nothingness
growing increasingly   smaller and
smaller and   smaller

by the mile marker before disappearing
into oblivion in
our rearview mirrors. Let's drive until all
our
stress withers away like the newspaper
memories

inside the fireplace of our Souls. Let's
drive until our map has no more roads
left, even
those few left undiscovered.
And if we have to let's drive to the
moon—as star after
glimmering star bounces off our
windshield

like a soothing afternoon rain.
But what about our responsibilities?
They'll
just be waiting for us when we get back.

So she said, "Then let's never take
our foot off the gas."

I closed the notebook and for a moment tried
valiantly to avoid looking Darlene in the eyes for
fear of an unfavorable reaction. But eventually

curiosity got the better of me and I snuck a peek in her direction. She was crying.

"Are you okay?" I asked.

She nodded her head and started to produce a weak smile, "Yes! That was so beautiful. It was a little pessimistic, but optimistic at the same time. Did you write that for someone? Who is the *she* you reference in it?"

"I did. I was a little infatuated with a friend of mine my first year of college, I'm not going to lie. But she only saw me as a brother to her and nothing more. Anyway, she had a really unrelenting quality about her in believing in endless *possibilities* despite the many obstacles life always seems to throw at us. There was just something about her way of thinking that I wish I could force myself to adopt."

She started to cry again and grabbed a hold of my hands, "That's so beautiful, Jackson. Did you love her?"

"I did. But she never wanted anything more than just a friendship. Last I knew she was still out chasing new possibilities. Heard she recently got engaged."

"I'm sorry that it didn't work out. Do you still talk with her?"

"No, she transferred to another school in another state last year. I haven't heard from her since."

Darlene inched closer to me on the bed and wrapped her arms around me. I could smell the beautiful aroma of her perfume and instantly I felt relaxed. I hadn't thought about Laura in ages, even though subconsciously a lot of my poetry wound up centering on her. Darlene had this mystical power to wash her away from my memory.

I was completely fixated on Darlene's beautiful brown hair as it engulfed both of our faces when she began to pull away. She was still crying. But in that moment the two of us instantly connected, as if we both had experienced the heartache of longing for someone who didn't long for us in return. She'd felt every single word of my poem, just as I'd felt it when I first wrote it. She was likely the only other person I'd ever met who had felt something I'd felt.

She was a wounded bird like me, but a wounded bird that fell out of another tree. Our paths down to the ground were likely completely different, but the end result was the same. Somehow we'd found each other.

We gazed into each other's eyes for only a few seconds, but to me it felt like a lifetime. Her hazel eyes searched beyond the exterior of my brown eyes. They peered into my empty soul and latched on to the tattered twine of what was left of my emotions. And she wouldn't let go. That much I knew.

Darlene leaned in to me and placed her ruby red lips on mine. It was as if a tractor-trailer had hit me at full force. Some people talk about talk about seeing fireworks, or feeling butterflies in their stomach, or descending down the drop of a steep roller coaster but I felt like I was hit by a truck. And it was a sensational feeling.

It was unlike any feeling I'd ever experienced before. And I didn't want it to end.

Darlene gently guided me on to my back and eased her body on top of mine. She tore my shirt off and threw it into the pile of clothes already on the floor. She made her way from my lips to my neck to my chest and down my torso. In one fluid motion she tore my belt out of the loops and instantly started unzipping my pants.

It was all going so fast, that I could hardly process it. Before I knew it my boxers were around my ankles and I was inside her mouth.

I could hardly watch it felt so good. Every up and down motion of her bobbing head on my cock sent me into another world, a world in which I've rarely entered. I grabbed the pillow from behind me and placed it over my head to reduce the sexual shock I was falling under. It didn't help at all. If anything it made the sensation feel that much better.

Without warning I was greeted with a sudden warm sensation. She tossed the pillow away from my face and I looked down at her miraculous body to find that she was completely naked and thrusting her vagina up and down on my cock. She did a complete 180 from the woman she was ten minutes ago. All this time she was a porn star in an innocent girl's clothing.

I wish I could say that I have fond memories of the rest of that night, but it all happened so fast that that's all that I can recall. Sex, at least good sex, can be such a blur sometimes. The rest of our little tryst was such a fantastic mishmash of euphoria that I completely disappeared during it. I've never experienced sex of that quality before in my life that it basically took me to a place outside of my body. It was a remarkable sensation, one that I'm not sure I'll ever be able to experience again.

We lay there in bed for hours afterwards just talking. We talked about everything from work to poetry to art to our future plans. There was no limit on our conversation. It was the happiest I'd been in a long time.

But when it was finally over, something inside of me changed. I knew I'd met the missing piece to my life's puzzle. Darlene was my other half. But as she put on her clothes and we walked to my dorm room door I couldn't help but think about what falling in love with her might do to me. I've fallen in love before and it sucks. It hurts unlike anything in this world when it doesn't work out. And I can only imagine it hurts so much more when it falls apart with someone who complements who you are better than anyone you've ever met.

I can't have Darlene in my life. She doesn't want to leave this part of the country, and I want nothing to do with this area for as long as I live. She wants to be a teacher like her mother. I want to be a writer and bask in the big city lights of Hollywood and travel the world from book signing to book signing.

As beautiful as she is inside and out, I don't want to be stuck in a rut that I can't possibly get out of. And I'm afraid of not being able to get out.

I wrapped her sweater around her shoulders and kissed her on the cheek. She grabbed a hold of my hand.

She stared at me for a moment and asked me in a broken tone, "Jackson, will I ever see you again?"

I tossed the question back and forth in my mind even though I'd been thinking about it ever since we got out of bed and got dressed.

I looked her straight into her beautiful brown eyes and whispered, "No."

And with the unfortunate confirmation of that remark she lowered her eyes and let go of my hand before turning around and heading down the stairs toward the parking lot.

I wanted to stop her. I wanted to reassure her and tell her that somehow, someway, everything could all work out like some farfetched Nicholas Sparks romance novel. I wanted to tell her that our feelings for each other were more than just a physical attraction; that we were meant for each other. But I knew my life didn't work out that way. My life was a Shakespearean tragedy on its best day; it's just one disappointment after another.

I watched her beautiful body disappear into the distance. Never in my life had I ever wished I could throw away everything I'd ever worked for and just go with my heart. A part of me wanted to make this moment the lone exception, but my feet wouldn't move. I'm a week from graduation. I can't let a girl change my path. I can't let a girl come between me and my dreams. I can't let a girl keep me here.

Even in the off chance that it might be true love that I'm passing on.

Guildford University's Graduation Day was an absolute waste of three hours. But at the same time, I almost didn't want it to end. Four years of pure bliss and unforgettable memories away from Belmont. And now I'm being forced out into the real world for good. It almost doesn't even seem fair. This place has been my refuge for four years. The only place that ever made any sense to me. The only place that allowed me to forget about the life I was trying to leave behind. Now what do I do?

I'd finally earned my expensive piece of paper to frame and put up on whatever wall I plan to call my own for the next portion of my life's timeline. And nobody showed up to celebrate this milestone with me.

Well, no one that mattered anyway.

I ran into Colton on the side of the freeway. But it wasn't the Colton I remember. He was different. He was colder. And he didn't appear to recognize me at first.

He kept pointing toward the road ahead of me. I looked but saw nothing but endless miles of cracked concrete and plain scenery. There was nothing in front of me to marvel at, but Colton kept pointing.

"What are you pointing at?" I asked.

He looked at me but said nothing. He pulled a folded note from his pocket and handed it to me. Before I could even open it to look at it, I glanced back at the road and back at Colton.

"What's out there?" I asked right as he disappeared.

I looked down at the paper in my hand and opened it up and scribbled in Colton's handwriting was the simple message: *Keep moving toward the horizon.*

I woke up in a cold sweat to a storm brewing outside my apartment window. I lay in bed staring absentmindedly up at my ceiling thinking about every detail of the dream. I don't know what it all meant, if it meant anything.

But it was good to see Colton again, even if it was only in a dream.

There's nothing I hate more than my job at the convenient store. It's the furthest thing from what I intended to be doing with my life after college. I'm the proud owner of a nearly $60,000 piece of paper, and I'm doing nothing with my life that pertains to writing or my minor of teaching.

Some life.

Day in and day out it's the same old story. A fresh out of college twenty-something barely scraping by on minimum wage to afford a shitty ass apartment in Lewisfield, North Carolina. Just living the fucked up American dream.

But at least I wasn't back in Belmont having to deal with my parents anymore. Sure, they forgave me and everything for what I put them through last Christmas, and I forgave them for not showing up to my graduation, but I knew deep down that I didn't want to have to deal with them for any longer than I had to. So I made the decision to move away and see where the road takes me. Colton's dream had to have meant something after all. There's nothing for me in Belmont, so why stay? I've just got to keep moving toward the horizon.

Lewisfield may not be the tourist destination of the east coast, but it's better than Belmont. Something will change for the better I'm sure. Good things just take time. I just hope these good things arrive sooner rather than later.

I glided along the pavement as my hair blew wildly behind me. My left arm stretched forever out the window caressing the breeze like a long lost lover. While my fingers played harmonies with the wind weaving in and out through its calming current.

The road in front of me was seemingly endless. A never-ending straightaway toward parts unknown. Road signs try to inform me where I'm heading, but they offer no accurate mileage. No indication of when I'll get there. Wherever the hell *there* is.

The first sign I see has a robin perched upon the peak. It reads: **Happiness** – *Miles Ahead.*

The numbers had fallen off onto the ground. I had no idea how far ahead Happiness was, but as long as I'm headed for Happiness, I can't imagine the journey will be anything but enjoyable. Who cares how many miles are between my destination and me? Who cares how long it takes me, as long as I get there?

The concrete beneath me began to break a part. The road started to sink and fall away from view. My car was floating. At least it felt like floating. The road signs disappeared only slightly. The destination had been changed from Happiness to Unclear. Everything went black. I started to fall rapidly toward the abyss below me.

I landed in a hallway at a building I vaguely remember. A place I couldn't wait to leave. A job I couldn't stand having. But I was on my way toward newer and brighter horizons. Or so I thought.

"Are you willing to relocate?" asked the static disembodied voice on the other end of the receiver.

"*Immediately,*" I responded without hesitation as I rubbed the velvet lettering on my grey high school alma mater shirt.

The final moments of the phone interview that changed my career-less life forever plays on a constant loop within my nightly dreams. Every night I relive this scene, among others. I'm not sure if it should be considered a dream or a nightmare. It haunts me nevertheless. Whenever I dream about school, or anything that led me to my current profession, I wake up in a cold sweat from utter terror. This morning was no different. If only Colton could revisit my dreams and point me again toward the horizon I'm destined for. Why can't I get that call for my manuscript selling? My writer dreams are dwindling by the day.

Sometimes I wonder if I made the right choice. Is this truly what I *want* to do? A part of me wishes I'd said no to teaching and continued working odd end jobs while searching for the perfect publisher for my first novel. I mean, can I really make a difference in anybody's life after all? How can I be a role model when I don't even have my own life together?

I'm a teacher.

Teaching: A once immensely heralded, highly regarded profession, now turned illegitimate stepchild of all that's wrong with the 21st century. My mind often recalls a cartoon satirically comparing the late 1960s with the present day. The first frame, 1969, depicts two parents and a confident teacher asking a child to "Explain these bad grades." The second frame, present day, has two parents demanding their child's disheveled teacher to "Explain these bad grades," while the child stands stoically, arms crossed with a smug appearance of self-righteous victory on his face. Such an accurate depiction of how the times and mindsets have drastically changed in regard to education.

And honestly, it's complete bullshit.

Yes, I'm a teacher. Every day I regret becoming one a little more.

There are two different types of teachers, those who truly make a difference in children's lives and were born to teach, and those who are in the profession for all the wrong reasons. Those reasons vary with each individual.

In my three years of teaching, I haven't met the first kind of teacher. Sure, I had a few when I was younger whom I absolutely adored, who may have had an impact on my decision to ultimately pursue teaching. Not because I necessarily wanted to teach, but because I wanted to be like them. They were the type of individuals who made your life better without you even knowing it at the time. Those people who are so unique and innovative that you cling on their every word and discover things about yourself that you never knew. They make you believe deeper in yourself and push you to strive for things you never thought were a possibility before you met them.

But I'm not sure those kind of teachers exist anymore. It's a dying breed, as rare as a chance encounter with the likes of Bigfoot.

Of that species of teacher who teaches for all the wrong reasons, there are numerous sub-species. All of whom I have had the unfortunate pleasure of getting to know quite well during my three year tenure as an educator at North Grayson High School in northwest Florida. They're like an infection that won't go away no matter how much you apply the prescribed ointment the doctor assured you would work. They just keep multiplying like unsightly sores on the face of education.

The first sub-species: *The drunk*. He's the old standby who's been around since the beginning of time. He probably should have retired by now, but he can't afford to because he's wasted all of his money over the years on booze and most recently the settlement in his divorce. You can smell the whiskey on his breath, even at 6:55 in the morning. The only way he gets through the excruciating tribulations of the day, is by taking swigs from the flask hidden in his desk drawer in between classes.

The druggie. More concerned with being every student's friend than their teacher. Often smokes with his students after school and is the mastermind behind a school wide drug-trafficking ring. Won't actually have a legitimate opinion on anything, unless of course it's about America's need to wake up and finally legalize recreational drug use.

The pervert. The well-presented fashionista who works out far more than any human being rightly needs to, who all the girls have a crush on. He secretly has crushes on them as well. Far more interested in hearing what his female students have to say than the males, and finds enjoyment catching glimpses down his busty students shirts every chance he gets. He'll likely wind up in prison someday for having sex with one or more of his students.

The home-wrecker. Like a wounded cougar she seeks out the most vulnerable of male teachers and attempts to ruin every inch of his pathetic life. A provocative dresser, who bends but never breaks and deliberately teases any man who shows her the least bit of interest. The opposite gender is like putty in her hands. Once she's destroyed every bit of her newest preys' masculinity and every shred of his reputation with each soul-sucking kiss dripping from her pursing lips, she moves right on to the next poor sap who knows nothing of her wicked powers.

The Nazi. Also known as the "Know-it-all" or "Good God, I hate that bitch." She has her nose in everything, and is not even the slightest bit interested in making friends with anybody. She is convinced that because she knows people, that she has more authority than anyone else. She is the dictator in what's supposed to be a democracy. Although only a teacher, she pretends to be an administrator and will tell you everything you're doing wrong, and nothing you're doing right. You should be so lucky to be on her good side.

The ass-kisser. Not much different from the Nazi, but far less deliberate in trying to piss you off, at least to your face. Whereas the Nazi will bluntly tell it like it is, the ass-kisser will willingly talk behind your back so as to avoid any immediate confrontation. She is a slithering snake valiantly attempting on every occasion to maneuver her way up the authoritarian ladder of success, and will shove anyone in front of the bus if it helps out her own cause. She plays nice in public, but stacks the deck in her favor behind closed doors.

And then there's *Purgatorio*. Someone in "limbo" with no true *one* distinction. Like a lost puppy, they don't know who they are, or why they do what they do; the most intriguing yet mysterious of the sub-species of teachers. That's me. I'm in Purgatory and I don't quite know how to get out.

Every morning on my drive to work I met the gaze of this homeless man on the corner of my street and Loman Parkway. We would always experience this minute long stare off that rarely saw either of us blink.

I'd usually nod at him and he'd usually nod at me. Not much of an interaction, but significant to my every day nonetheless.

When it came to homeless men, he was probably the most put together of all the ones I'd seen anticipating handouts. His clothes showed some sign of aging and lack of cleanliness, but they weren't tattered and falling apart like most. He had a checkered suit jacket and wore a loose fitting tie around his neck and leaned up against the bus stop bench with his head rested on his bag and his cardboard sign rested against his leg.

I couldn't help but picture myself in his weathered shoes, begging for spare change on the crowded intersection of a major highway. He could very well be my future. Hell, maybe he is a teacher, or was; just a down on his luck former educator with broken dreams, starving, life in shambles, hoping for just one thing to go right.

It certainly wouldn't surprise me. I know it's just a matter of time before I'm sitting right beside him sharing the last sip of backwash soda from the Big Gulp we found in the trashcan.

Due to the overwhelming influx of dreadful educators who care a little less each passing year with paychecks waning and obnoxious students waxing, American education is at its lowest point. Intellectually, there's something wrong with *all* of us, I fear. It's almost as if, while the years have been laboriously moving forward, we as an "educated" human race have been drifting farther out to sea like a lonely volleyball ripped from the grasp of our emaciated FedEx owner's hands.

We're just plummeting down the throngs of the evolutionary ladder into a massive heap of our own smoldering feces. And we're surprisingly *okay* with it, it seems.

We have been so accustomed to having things handed to us that we no longer feel the need to work for anything. We even bring our own children up this way. I have *lived* the second frame of that satirical cartoon far too often. I cannot tell you how many times my students have asked me questions about their grades after they have received an interim report for their parents to sign or an end-of-quarter report card, as if *I'm* the one who is at fault when *they don't try*.

As that cartoon suggests, I am responsible for their bad grades. I guess I didn't make the material interesting enough. I evidently am at fault for supplying adequate notes from which to study, and that clearly caused my students to Christmas tree every fucking answer on the test in which they completed in a whopping **five** minutes. You're right, all *my* fault. My apologies. I will try to do better next time.

It runs like a recurring sitcom in my head that I've grown bored with because I know every line uttered by every character.

"Mr. Cain, why did you give me a C+?"

I could feel my blood boil with intense indignation, "I, beg your pardon?"

Holly tapped her toe out of frustration, as if I were deliberately trying to avoid answering her, and responded impishly, "I *said*, why did you give me a C+ in your class this past quarter? Why couldn't you just bump it up to a B-?"

Apparently I'm in the business of handing out raises for minimal effort. It's tough to prepare teens for real life when they seem to think that by not doing their work they still deserve to reap the benefits of success.

"I'm sorry, Holly…" I started, and began to see the edges of her mouth curl into a Grinch-like smile, "…would you care to *rephrase* that line of questioning?"

Her smile disappeared almost as quickly as my monthly paycheck.

"I don't understand…"

Of course you don't, you only managed a C+ average in my fucking class. What you should have led with was, 'Mr. Cain, how is it that I *earned* a C+?'

Kids these days come to school with an undeserved sense of entitlement. It's as if they feel they are pre-celebrity status and should simply be given good grades and advanced diplomas so that they can focus on the more important things in life like their rap careers, or being on the newest season of *16 and Pregnant.* It's a sad reality.

But as Kurt Vonnegut once said, "so it goes."

I was able to coast through my first two years of teaching. It was a brand new adventure through uncharted territory that I was anxious to explore. Every day was a joyous experience, whether it was a good day or a bad day, as each morning I couldn't wait to get to my classroom and start preparing for the next lesson.

But that unmatched excitement gradually disappears in every teacher. In some it takes decades to dissipate. In others it takes little to no time to begin its permanent retreat. Everything turned sour as my third year of teaching slowly progressed.

I no longer enjoyed being in my classroom. In fact, I dreaded entering it every morning. I can't tell you how many times I daydreamed on my way to work that an act of God took out my classroom overnight. I would turn the key to my door and open it up to see a miraculous sight of scattered papers and burnt furniture and a gigantic gaping hole in the side of the building, as bits and pieces of a burning meteor still clung to life setting fire to any remaining morsel of what was once my English classroom. I used to show up an hour and a half before school started in anticipation of the newest school day. I didn't even get paid for that additional time. That's how excited I was to be there. Now, I tend to stroll in four minutes late mere seconds shy of the 7 o'clock warning bell, with disheveled bedridden hair and a coffee in my hand.

"Good morning Mr. Cain! Ooh, did we have a rough weekend?" asked the way-too-chipper-on-a-Monday-morning attendance monitor behind the front counter as I begrudgingly signed in on the clipboard. My name was one of the last staff boxes that remained empty.

"Rough *life* is more like it," I responded with little self-assurance.

I was mere inches away from the lobby door to Hell when a voice bellowed above all others, "Someone doesn't look happy to be here."

I knew that voice. I *hated* that voice. If chalkboards were still used in contemporary classrooms, her voice would be the equivalent of the age-old analogy of nails on a chalkboard. I instead classify her voice more accurately as the cringe-worthy sound that Styrofoam typically makes.

"What's the matter? Can't even acknowledge me? You're *late*, you know."

"I'm aware of that Jasmine."

"Excuse me? I'm your superior. It's Mrs. Raker to you, and don't you forget it."

Her shrill falsetto cut through my eardrums like a knife.

"Forgive me, Mrs. Raker. Where *are* my manners?" I hoped she was astute enough to pick up on my deliberate sarcasm.

"Probably at home with your clean wardrobe. I can't believe you came to work looking like *that*. My God, you look like a hobo."

Apparently not. I shot a quick glare from above my sunglasses and politely replied, "Thanks for the confidence boost, Mrs. Raker."

"Whatever. Anyway, I'm glad I caught you. Don't forget that today is my Teacher Leader day, so I will be coming into your fourth period class to observe. You better have something good prepared for me to observe."

This news hit me like a freight train careening off the tracks at 100 mph.

Fuck me, I completely forgot, "There's like two days left in the school year, what do you think?"

She shrugged off my remark and as I pushed open the door, turned the corner and headed out of the main lobby I caught a quick glimpse of the intense satisfaction in Jasmine's eyes as she undoubtedly noticed the sheer surprise in mine.

T he walk to my classroom was like a funeral procession. The farther I walked, the more depressing it became. My classroom was situated in the most remote part of the building and I frequently noticed the expressions of the teachers gradually getting less and less elated and more and more miserable as I approached my room. My hallway felt like the city morgue. And I was just the lonely undertaker.

Not even before my hand grazed the door handle to my room the bell rang and the vast ocean of students began pouring down the hallway with the "serious student" minority leading the charge and getting to class in a fairly quick manner. They were followed by the overwhelming masses of the "why am I forced to be in this prison" majority. I don't even bother to go in to my room anymore when I arrive late, I simply open the door and stand there waiting for my first block students to show up.

I've always enjoyed listening to the conversations of the many students walking by my door though. Intellectual conversations have always been scarce. Usually I get complete nonsense and utter annihilation of the English language.

It's tough being a teacher in the ever-changing 21st century. It's even more difficult when you're an English teacher. Every word a student utters gets assessed, critiqued, and constantly corrected in an English teachers mind. You would think getting a verbal snafu corrected numerous times would eventually ignite a trigger in the back of a student's mind to finally realize that what they've been saying is grammatically incorrect and needs to be fixed immediately. *You would think.*

The English language is falling apart and is drastically taking a nosedive into premature oblivion. I don't even know what the hell my kids are talking about anymore. If only the new paint job and random updates on the school's grounds could eliminate our mediocre reputation and encourage a more sophisticated and goal-oriented student body to want to attend it. Then there might be some hope for the future.

"Nigga, quit flaggin', she ratchet!"

A more sophisticated student body. Right, *if only.*

"Aye bruh, that trippin' bitch be hella fake."
Yup, the cream of the crop right here in my midst.

Every day I'm surrounded by these quips and phrases that are an all too accurate illustration of the sad demographic of the modern student, summarized in one pathetic excuse for a conversation.

"Bruh, for real do', listen 'ere she straight tappin'. She know she want that D."

If there is a just and merciful God, you will kill me now.

Four years removed from living under my parents' roof and still I'm surrounded by a bunch of fucking idiots. With every swig of my coffee I can't help but wish it was something stronger, perhaps a life-threatening bottle of Everclear 180 proof.

They're breeding a special species of apathetic teacher in the 21st century who simply do not care whether they're ineffective or come highly touted. Whether they make an everlasting impact on students or cause them to seek therapy for the remainder of their lives. We aren't given any indication that we're valued at all, and in my brief tenure as an educator I can't recall one time where *anyone*, student, parent, colleague, whomever has ever told me "thank you for doing what you do." How can we be expected to strive toward being the highly effective teacher who makes a difference in every student's life when not a shred of gratitude is ever offered? What's my motivation if I'm only likely to reach one in every ten kids I teach? Now, I'm no whiz at math but even I know that making a difference in the lives of three students in a class size of 30 isn't the greatest percentage of success stories.

Say what you will about me but they don't pay me enough to care. I make barely enough money to get by, while athletes and politicians make more than they can manage. They basically drown in their wealth while I struggle to stay afloat. I've been told that money is the root of all evil, but I'd be lying if I said I didn't want a little of the devil inside me. We all do.

It's taken only three years to mold me into the type of teacher one becomes after nearly forty years on the job. *You know the type.* The teacher who knows their time is dwindling and who is only eyeing retirement and the monetary package that accompanies it. That small morsel of incentive one receives for stepping down and letting the district save massive amounts of cash by packing up their belongings and hiring some naïve little prick who knows nothing of the headaches of contemporary education.

It's taken me three years to realize that modern education is bullshit when only a small fraction of students even want to earn a diploma.

My advice to college students majoring in Education: get out while you still have a discernible pulse. Get out while you still care about others. When I was in college they pumped sunshine down our throats and told us how remarkable it is to be able to enlighten and inspire future generations of students.

It all sounded so beautiful, so encapsulating, that is until you were put in front of the students you were expected to enlighten and inspire, wondering how in the world some of them even made it through life this long.

Every year I get a new batch of students. Every year I hate my life a little more. I can pick out the faces of the students I imagine will make something of themselves. Those individuals are few and far between. I can also pick out the students who will likely be on the evening news for committing criminal acts or for suffering an untimely death, and those students who I'll probably come across on porn websites.

I'm supposed to enlighten those who can't even spell *enlighten*? I'm supposed to enlighten those who truly don't want to *be* enlightened? At least not by me, or any other teachers. They have already made their choices about where their lives are going before even walking into my classroom.

The last couple days of school I rarely teach anything. I hand my students some study guides for their final exam, which the majority of them don't even realize that 90% of the final exam questions and answers are in the study guide, word for word, and I let them sit there and study with it the entire class. And by study, I mean most of them sit there on their phones, rather than actually utilizing their time effectively.

I usually like to start random conversations with some of them and see where they plan to be in the future, having a career or in college, starting a family and what not, kind of my last-ditch effort to see if my initial predictions about what their futures will be like are accurate or not.

"Laquesha, what do you want to do with your life when you're finished with school?" I asked one of my first block students who was busted for a dress code violation for probably the fiftieth time this year.

"I don' know, I'm prolly jus' gon' be a strippa' downtown at Peeper's," she replied in a tone of complete sincerity.

But I vaguely caught the glimmer of despair behind the glint in her eyes. Deep down she probably wants to be something more, but she doesn't know how to get it. And I don't know how to help her find it. It's a never-ending game of cat and mouse.

"Trenton, what about you?"

"You don't wanna know Mr. Cain."

"Actually," I started, "I kind of do. What are your plans when you're out of here?"

He looked me square in the eye, pulled out a yellow and red bandana and tied it around his face. My gut feeling from the beginning of the year that he was associated with a gang was now confirmed.

"There's only two outcomes for me. Death or prison."

The calmness and sincerity in his voice shook me to my core. He'd clearly already come to terms with what his future was bound to be. And it pained me to realize that I'd likely see his picture pop up on my television screen in a few years no doubt for some breaking news story, either for committing a murder or getting killed.

I'm surrounded by the hopeless and the damned.

After all, I'm not Jesus. I can't work miracles. I can't walk on water, I can't turn water in to wine, I can't rise from the dead, and I can't convince these kids that their lives are worth more than they think, when even I don't believe it.

Teachers aren't miracle workers, like former teacher turned poet Taylor Mali once preached in a pre-school training YouTube video. You have to have the drive to succeed instilled in you by the time you get to high school, otherwise we're in a hopeless endeavor. It's the physically disabled leading the legally blind. I can't create something in you that you kicked out of the apartment complex of your mind when you made the transition from child to teen. When you went from endless dreamer, believing you could be anything to feeling convinced that the whole world was out to get you and you'd never amount to anything more than your deadbeat dad who walked out on your family when you were born.

Once your inner drive is pushed aside, it's gone. And it's damn near impossible to get back.

The clock ticked away each meaningless second of life as fourth period swiftly approached. Only one lousy week left of school and Mrs. Raker insisted on observing my every move for one last time.

What could she possibly see that she hasn't already seen the last five times she observed me? Is anyone at their highest level of performance this close to the end of the school year? She's going to be gravely disappointed, as she usually is when my class is graced by her presence.

Every day I feel like my classroom is a tourist attraction. Administrators, district personnel, Mrs. Raker, and other guests apparently of significant importance constantly walk in and out of classes like it's a public petting zoo and that their presence is in no way a disruption of learning. All day long it's an in and out procession of tourists gawking at the zookeeper and the animals at feeding time. Tourists critiquing every move the zookeeper makes, every word the zookeeper utters, ready to pounce on every mistake rather than glorifying a single triumph.

One such visit probably a month or so ago, one of those tourists noted a criticism, which I received as feedback via email a week later: *Joey only answered three out of the six problems and appeared disengaged at times. This needs to be improved.*

I considered that more of a personal triumph in that: *Joey for the first time all year actually managed to answer three out of the six problems and finally remembered to put his name on his damn paper.* I wish I'd have emailed that back as my response.

You have to know the animals before you berate the zookeeper for how they handle them. You can't assume that minimal effort on a student's paper means the teacher isn't doing their job. Case in point, that minimal effort could have been more than that individual has put into an assignment all year. Progress doesn't just happen overnight. Contrary to the beliefs of educational governing bodies, progress takes time.

It's no wonder people go postal and shoot up grocery stores and shopping malls. A person can only hear so much criticism before they finally snap.

The bell chimed loudly as my second period students rushed into the hallways toward their next class. I wasn't even halfway out the door when I was greeted by a familiar face that snapped me back into reality and startled me into submission.

"Still looking like shit, I see."

It's a good thing I don't have a self-esteem issue.

"It's so wonderful to see you again too, Jas-," I was able to catch myself in time as I noticed her eyes twitching in a fit of hysterical anger, "Mrs. Raker."

She looked me dead in the eyes and I could see the hate boiling in her pupils. The deep hazel blanketing each iris appeared to have atomic bombs igniting a drastic change in the shade of their color. Jasmine had transformed from bitch to über-bitch in mere seconds.

"Listen here *Jack*, you'd better start to remember your place fairly quickly. You want to continue teaching at this school, or any school in the state of Florida for that matter, I'd start watching my tongue if I were you."

When I first began teaching, that little threat would have frightened me into making every attempt imaginable to clean up my act and impress this woman. But now, it doesn't even raise the hairs on the nape of my neck even slightly. All I want to do is get through this class period and the remaining week of school without killing someone or myself.

"I'll just add that to my ever-expanding To-Do list," I mumbled as she briskly walked into my room and hijacked the seat behind my desk, whipping out her red pen and yellow notepad. The gallows were set with the trapdoor primed to drop.

"Good morning class! Let's get those notebooks out and get our Daily Vocabulary word written down!" I bellowed with a little more gusto than was typical of me at this time of the year.

Already I saw Mrs. Raker frantically writing away out of the corner of my eye. No doubt, negative things.

"Today's word is *battle-ax*."

"What does it mean?" whined Carlos from the back of the room.

I closed my eyes in annoyance, hoping it wasn't etched across my face.

We've been in school for 177 days. All fucking year we've done this at the beginning of each class. I give them a word, they write it down. I give them that word in a sentence hoping that the context clues help them figure out the definition, which is usually the case, and they write down the definition we come up with. Simple.

"We're about to find out, Carlos," I managed to blurt out in as pleasant a tone as I could muster.

"Isn't it a weapon?" asked one of my more inquisitive students.

"It is, Janet," I responded shortly, "but in this sentence I'm about to give you, that's not the definition we'll be looking for. Here it is: *Jon's teacher Mrs. Baker can be a real battle-ax when it's her time of the month.*"

Mrs. Raker sprung to life from her notes, lifting her head from the pages in a frenzy. I caught a quick glance at the astonishment in her face, but I couldn't tell if it was due to the fact she knew what a battle-ax was, or if it was my off-color example that included a name that sounded eerily similar to hers.

"A bitch!" shouted Carlos.

"You're absolutely right, Carlos, a bitch! But let's put it into more school friendly terminology, shall we?"

"Oh, okay um, I guess mean and unpleasant?"

"Mean and unpleasant it is. Perfect definition, Carlos."

Mrs. Raker had apparently seen enough for her observation as she jolted out of her chair and raced out the door rolling her eyes at me in apparent disgust.

"Ladies and gentleman, the *battle-ax* has left the building."

The class broke in to uncontrollable laughter and for the first time in months, I felt like I had connected with a group of my students. Of course it was at the expense of someone else's feelings, but you'll have that now and then. And for the first time in probably longer than that, I actually laughed along with them and enjoyed my job. I haven't experienced many moments like this in a long while. Maybe I didn't need a bottle of Everclear 180 proof to survive my remaining school days after all.

A bottle of 150 proof would do just fine.

Some days I just can't deal with anyone's bullshit; students, colleagues, administrators, *anyone*. If God himself were to manifest into physical form and offer a consoling sentiment and a shoulder to lean on, I would politely say, "Go fuck yourself."

Sure, one class could go all right and keep my spirits up for a brief amount of time but ultimately once that class ends I'm brought back down to reality and forced to deal with anyone and everyone that I don't want to deal with. I know for a fact that Führer Raker was likely in an administrator's office expressing her disgust at my observation and my deliberate insults at her expense. They have already asked me to come back and teach next year, and regardless of my uncertainty I reluctantly said that I'd be back, but I'm almost positive a shit storm is on the horizon.

The only person I knew with any kind of ability to cheer me up was Perry, six doors down in the history hallway. We have the same lunch period every day directly after second block, but both of us can't stand the people we work with so we often eat alone. When either of us interrupts the other, it's usually because we want to bitch about something or someone.

The path to Perry's room is often an adventure in and of itself. I *hate* leaving my room for fear of the inevitable barrage of people. They're like vultures feeding on my rotting corpse in the middle of the hallway. Colleagues and students are always attempting to stop me and waste every second of my precious twenty-five minute lunch period with some bullshit sob story that I care nothing about.

In the thirty seconds it would take me to get to Perry's room, I feel like Walter Payton zigzagging my way through a choreographed teacher-student blitz designed to keep me from breaking the goal line of Perry's door.

I charged through the door like a wrecking ball demolishing the side of a condemned building and heard a nervous rustling from behind Perry's desk. In the split second I made it through the threshold of Perry's door, I caught a glimpse of a young girl jumping up from beneath the desk wiping her mouth as he frantically zipped up the front of his slacks.

Now I've known Perry to do some stupid shit in my three years working alongside him, but I can't even begin to believe what I just walked in on.

The embarrassed girl, unable to speak, rushed passed me and scurried out the door disappearing down the hallway, disheveled hair and all.

Normally, I have an appropriate response for everything. Sadly, they don't prepare you how to react to a situation such as this in Education courses in college. For the first time in my life, I was at a loss for words.

"Spit it out, fucker," Perry urged.

As an English teacher, all I could think of were the many different puns that would be suitable retorts given the pretense to this particular conversation starter.

"*Well?*"

I kept the childish puns to myself and managed to mumble, "What the fuck are you thinking? Was she doing what I *think* she was doing?"

"Yeah," he responded almost proudly, "she was sucking me raw."

"In school?"

"What? It heightens the pleasure, Jack, with the sheer risk of it all."

"But that was a student!"

"Get off my dick, she's legal."

"Okay? But the fact that she's your *student*, and not to mention the same age as your little sister doesn't, in any way, creep you the fuck out?"

"Not even remotely."

"You've got a problem, my friend."

"I've made peace with it."

"How long have you been doing this?"

"With *her*? That was probably the fourth or fifth time this year, I think."

"What do you mean '*with her*'? Do you mean to tell me that there have been others that you've done this shit with?"

"Of course, Jack! At least three or four others, this year alone."

"But why? Why would you put yourself in such a vulnerable situation?"

"Are you fucking kidding me? Have you seen some of these chicks?"

"Yes, I have," I replied, "but that doesn't –"

Perry lifted his hand to interrupt me, "Are you a faggot? You're telling me that you haven't once fantasized about sticking *little Jackson* inside one of your female students with tits the size of Christina Hendricks?"

"No, and no," I declared without hesitation.

"You have got to be shitting me! Not even once?"

"Not even once."

"Oh dude, you don't know what you're missing, Jack. I'll admit I was afraid when I first acted upon my sexual urges. The first time it happened was five years ago, in my first year of teaching. This huge breasted senior I had for study hall asked me to help her with an assignment she was having trouble with, so I told her that I would. She came over to my desk and sat right in my lap. Oh my God, Jack, you have no idea how silky smooth this girl's skin was. She was the perfect height to where her tits were practically in my mouth. Ugh, I didn't want her to get up but I felt just like you at the time that it was inappropriate, and I was about to ask her to politely get off my lap and sit in the chair beside me, but before I could spit it out she grabbed ahold of my crotch and whispered in my ear that she wanted to fuck me. After that moment, I learned that if you're discrete enough about it and take the necessary precautions, you're golden and can fuck whomever you want. And when they're of legal age, it's even better because it's less stress. I'm telling you, you've got to try it at least once."

I fumbled for the right words, "I don't even know what to say to that."

Perry leaned forward in his chair and pulled out a little black notebook and started rifling through the tattered pages, "What do you want a blonde, a brunette? Big tits? No tits? Small waist and a big ass? I could get you anything you want."

"Are you seriously trying to pimp out female students to me right now?"

Perry chuckled, "Well, you are looking a little flustered my friend. Some female companionship might do you good. That girlfriend of yours still playing with your cock or is she making you do it yourself these days?"

"I'm not about to have this conversation with you about my girlfriend."

"I'm just saying, you gotta let it out once in a while. Let little Jackson breathe."

"Fuck you," I joked.

"Fuck *me*? No, I will not have sex with you Jackson."

"You're such an asshole," I muttered but then paused as I had realized something that could have been problematic for Perry, "I was wondering, what if that hadn't been *me* bursting through your door just now? Like I mean, what if it were an administrator, or another teacher, or another student?"

I could tell right then that Perry hadn't even considered that as a possibility. The wheels appeared to be turning at an intense speed in his mind, and there was a faint look of fear for a brief moment.

"Shit, you're right Jack. That would have been a nasty situation. My ass would likely be out on the side of the road right now. Apparently, I'm not exercising *enough* precautions. I'll have to consider that for next year."

"Next year? You're going to continue doing this shit in school? You really should seek professional help. Maybe look into attending a Sex Addicts Anonymous meeting or something. I think they meet on Tuesday nights down at the YMCA."

"Sex Addicts Anonymous? That exists?"

"Yeah," I remarked, wondering where he was going with it.

"You might be on to something there, Jack. I'll have to check that out. Might be a great place to pick up chicks."

"Oh, for the love of God, I'm out of here."

"What? You know how my mind works, don't act surprised."

"You should think a little less with your cock and little more with your brain."

"I would, but it hurts too much."

Despite the compromising situation I found Perry in at the beginning of lunch, he still managed to ease my mood somehow. It's no wonder he's able to talk these young girls into doing sexual things with him. He has a way with his words and his demeanor is so domineering that he convinces you to trust him regardless of his track record of poor decisions and in this case, makes you forget that you caught him doing something completely unforgivable. Something that will likely see him sucking the devil's cock in the inner circles of Hell for all eternity.

"You need any copies made or anything, since I have planning next?"

"Fuck no. Jesus. What do you think I am a responsible teacher who actually plans shit? Quit flirting with me and get the hell out of here."

And with a feigning smile and a reluctant wave, I jolted out of Perry's classroom back into the trenches as the bell sounded for third block.

The break room is every teacher's safe haven.

Every once in a while we want to escape the clutches of the educational setting. Things get unbearable and when they do the building begins to sprout appendages to choke you with all of its might. It's like a game of tag and the break room is the neutral zone. It's impossible to escape from the educational setting in your own classroom or a colleague's classroom or the cafeteria or the hallway because everything reminds you that you're surrounded by students.

Except for the break room.

Except for that one neutral zone conveniently situated in every hallway that allows teachers to disappear, if only for a short time, and forget that there's such a thing as students.

This time however, I was trying to get away from everyone. People in general have been my kryptonite as of late, and a few moments of serenity within the calm confines of the break room is just what the doctor ordered.

She didn't even have to turn around for me to know it was her. The shape of that woman's behind as she leaned over the copier made it appear so immaculately crafted, I almost felt compelled to stop and sit down so that the blood could return to the rest of my body. Darrah Meadows was one of those women so intricately and uniquely put together that you could tell it was her body from a mile away. The curves of her 5'5" frame were clearly chiseled out of gold like a perfectly sculpted masterpiece. Every woman envied her, and every man wanted her.

"Hey there, Jackson," Darrah shot her pleasantry toward me as I entered the break room at the end of the English hallway.

"Ms. Meadows, it's a pleasure to see you."

"Oh, honey please, call me Darrah."

"With all due respect Ms. Meadows, I wouldn't feel comfortable calling you by your first name, at least not until I get to know you better."

"Well, aren't you a sweetheart," she grabbed her copies and moved closer to where I was situated near the door, "I guess, I might just have to let you get to know me better then." As she made her way out the door her hand nestled upon my chest and she dragged it down to the front of my thigh near the side of my crotch. I could smell the sweet sensation of sensuality emitting from Darrah's body as she left the break room. Never in my life had I felt so alive yet so cheap at the same time.

The break room in the English hallway was hardly ever used. It was so far removed from the frenzy of the rest of the building that no one ever wanted to use it. The only people I knew that frequented it often were myself and Bill Starks. Sure enough as I opened the door to the lounge, there he sat Al Bundy-esque on the divan at the edge of the room, staring into the abysmal haze that exists in all of us, sipping periodically from his trusty flask.

"Good morning Bill."

"Good? What's good about it?" he exclaimed rather sullenly.

I guess I couldn't really fault him for having asked such a question, as I likely would not have been able to answer with any degree of positivity.

"How's life treating you these days?" I implored as I made my way to the refrigerator for a beer but found only water.

"You know that feeling you get when you pass a kidney stone?"

"Um," I started, perplexed, "having never actually passed a kidney stone, I'd have to say *no*?"

"Well then, just imagine something that's bigger than your urethra being pushed out of it at full force," he waited for a minute, "are you picturing it?"

"Unfortunately."

"That's how life's treating me these days, Jack. I feel like I'm constantly passing a kidney stone. Ain't that a sonuvabitch?" Bill proclaimed as he downed another large gulp from his flask.

"Ouch. I'm sorry to hear that."

"Not as sorry as I am, I'm afraid."

We sat in relative tranquility for a few moments before my need to eliminate the silence grew overwhelming.

"So what is it that's got you down, Bill? If you don't mind my asking."

At first he acted like he couldn't hear me, but as I continued to prod him with my piercing stare he eventually caved and cleared his throat, "I don't want to bore you with the shortcomings of my life, Jack."

"I'm sure it's not as bad as you think. Give it a shot. It might be therapeutic to get whatever's on your mind out in the open," I replied confidently.

"What are you a shrink in your spare time?" Bill asked.

I got a kick out of that and chuckled tenderly, "No, but now that I think about it, it might not be a bad gig. People talking to you about their problems might actually make you feel better about your own."

Bill let out a sarcastic groan, "I think I'd rather be the shrink then, instead of the patient. The only way for me to forget about my problems is by drinking."

"That works for a while, yeah, but eventually booze won't have any effect either. Just humor me Bill, maybe I can make you feel better."

Bill's groans grew louder and more reluctant, but just in the way he caved earlier he caved once again knowing full well he wouldn't be able to get rid of me that easily.

"Fine, what the hell. What do you want to know?"

"What do you want to tell me?" I inquired.

"No, don't do what we do to our students by answering a question with a question. I'm not a child who can be fooled, Jack. I'm old enough to be your grandfather. What do you want to know, why I'm an overweight, miserable drunk, who can't find it in his heart to finally retire and put this part of his life behind him?"

"Actually," I began, "that's probably an ideal place to start."

Bill grunted loudly and shrugged off my remark, "Look, I know you're young, but everybody has rough patches. So I don't feel bad asking you. Did you ever wake up one day Jack, and just wonder where you went wrong with your life?"

I thought about it for a second even though I knew I didn't have to think about it at all, as I had woke up this morning with that very thought, "Yeah, I have."

"How do you feel in those moments, when you're contemplating every choice you've ever made, that's had a profound impact in leading you to where you are now?"

"Honestly?"

"Please."

"I feel like shit."

Bill looked at me with a distinct gaze of immense satisfaction. I don't believe that he was satisfied with how I felt in those particular moments, but feeling more of a satisfaction in that I knew what he was experiencing firsthand. Nobody wants to spill his or her guts to somebody who's led a perfect, happiness-driven existence, somebody who cannot possibly relate to any emotion in which the speaker is describing.

"That's how I feel every day of my life, Jack. Sure, I've had some crowning moments early on in my life and my career. But I'm afraid we all reach a point where we start to fall apart. The Jenga tower that is our life is always but a millimeter away from collapsing. And mine is teetering on the brink of destruction."

"But why?" I interjected, "What's so off-kilter with your life that's pushing you and everything about your life over the edge?"

Bill looked worn and dejected, "Do you know *why* I drink?"

"To forget about your problems," I answered assuredly.

He smirked with a shred of titillation, "Ah, you *were* listening, you'd make a fair shrink I believe. But I meant more specifically, the reasons why I drink. Do you have any idea what my problems are?"

"Honestly, no. I really don't delve too much into the personal affairs of my colleagues."

"As rightfully you shouldn't. It's not that important, really. Too many teachers concern themselves far too much with the affairs of others. They get so consumed with everyone else's problems and then in time they're inheriting those same problems that weren't even theirs to begin with. Sure, they'll lie to you and say that it's because they *care* about everyone they work with, but they don't. They just want to make sure that everyone else's life is as bad as or worse than theirs. Why else do you think I go out of my way to relax in this teacher's lounge as opposed to all the others?"

"Probably for the same reason I do."

"I like to just get away from the congestion from the rest of the building. It relaxes me. Puts my mind at ease," he calmly reflected.

"But is that why you drink? That can't possibly be what contributes to any stress within your life?"

"No, no, that's not why I drink. At least not anymore," Bill fell quiet for a few minutes, and I was unsure if I should press him further on the matter, or simply let him collect his thoughts. Eventually he mustered up the courage to continue, "did you know I was married?"

"I didn't."

"Just shy of 40 years. We tied the knot around the same time I started teaching."

"And that's led to your excessive drinking?" I asked, genuinely confused at first and not quite following where Bill was headed with his remarks until a thought hit me like a freight train, "Oh, my God. I'm so sorry, Bill. When did your wife pass away?"

Bill looked at me with a faint amount of disgust, but that disgust was drowned out through the teary eyes he was struggling to hide.

"She didn't pass away, Jack. She left me. I came home one day and she was gone, along with half of the stuff in the house. It's one thing to feel like your coming home to an empty house when you're not on good terms with your wife. It's something completely different when you come home to an empty house because it's exactly that…empty. My wife of nearly 40 years left me high and dry."

"But why? She must have stated a reason, right? How could someone leave another person after such a long time being committed to them?" I asked dumbfounded.

Bill peered at me through his tear-soaked hands, "Sometimes, people just fall out of love. And we're forced to move on."

"No, I refuse to believe that."

"I can understand your unwillingness to accept that, Jack. I felt it myself for a while. You believe that either you always love someone or you never did. But a small fraction of the time, maybe, some individuals loved another person so completely that after a while all the love that they had to give, simply dried up and disappeared. It's a sad reality, I'm not denying that. Unfortunately I don't have the answers as to why this happens. Neither do you. It just does. Wives leave their husbands every day for that very reason, and vice versa."

"It's just not fair to you though. Nobody deserves to go through pain like that," I told him as reassuringly as I could manage, even as my voice began to crack.

"I appreciate that sentiment, Jack. But I doubt if there's truly anything that you could say that would mend the broken pieces of my heart," Bill declared solemnly as he frantically grabbed his flask and tilted the remaining fluids into his mouth.

We sat in relative silence for a few minutes that felt like hours. Bill appeared to be calm and collected despite having released a fair amount of feelings he'd been bottling up for quite a while. I wondered how long he'd been putting on this acting job. Although everyone knew he was a closet drunk, for the most part he was a well-respected, likeable guy who always had a smile etched on his face. I guess you never can tell what a person's going through simply by looking at them. Although I'm pretty good at picking out what will happen to people in the future, I'm awful at figuring out what's happened in people's pasts. Who knew Bill Starks came with so much baggage?

As the seconds continued to tick away and last block loomed, Bill eventually collected himself, stood up haphazardly and warily made his way for the door.

"You see this smile, Jack?" Bill asked as he briskly turned my way putting a professional looking grin upon his face, "Look at it, I mean, really *look* at it. It looks genuine doesn't it? Well, now you know that it isn't real. This is the smile of someone who is completely unhappy. Someone completely broken.

This is the smile that covers it all up, the smile that's job is to hide every ounce of sorrow. I'm just a really good actor. I always have been. Hollywood ain't got nothing on me."

And with that final remark, Bill was one step closer to the hallway, re-entering the world that was his Broadway stage.

The day from there on out seemed to drag like a prisoner pulling a ball and chain through the dirt in the prison fields. I wish I could say that fourth block had cheered me up. I wish I could say that I cared if fourth block even learned anything. But I don't. It's the end of the year. They don't care. They just want to do their time and call it a ten-month sentence.

Out of those ten months of the school year where students are forced to be in the classroom, I would wager my life savings on the fact that the overwhelming majority of the student body only *cares* about their academic success for a total of eight days.

That's four days for midterms and four days for finals.

The rest of the year is all meaningless white noise to them. They hate school. Sure, they love it for the social aspect and for the afterschool activities supplied to them through athletic teams and clubs, but that's it. That's all school means to them. Who gives a shit about grades? Who's dating who is far more important. Who has the newest kicks and the freshest look is far more important. They don't cherish the idea of school like third world children do. Why should they? It's always been readily available to them. They haven't had to fight for their life through devastating civil wars, crippling poverty, and incessant hunger.

The only time I have ever seen communities of people actively seeking change and actually caring about schools and all of the people in them are when a tragedy strikes. It's a shame that this country needs to be face to face with the end results of a horrifyingly debilitating catastrophe, *just to care.*

Perhaps if we had a school shooting at North Grayson things might change. Maybe people would *care* a little more. Hell, maybe *I'd* care a little more.

Perhaps if I initiated a social experiment, and took a couple casualties along the way by holding one of my English classes' hostage, the atmosphere might change around here. I could enact a new age version of Stephen King's *Rage.*

Forget the possible scenario of a crazy and deranged, socially misunderstood and emotionally unhinged student leading the charge. The teacher is easily the most unstable individual in any classroom. We're all just sticks of dynamite waiting to explode at any given moment.

You cannot imagine the amount of times I have daydreamed throughout the duration of the school year about bringing a firearm to school. You see all of these news stories about bullied kids with undiagnosed mental issues massacring students and teachers at their school in a fit of momentary rage, getting their images plastered all over the television while inciting another pointless discussion about gun control and the effects of mental illness and poor upbringing. Yet, you rarely hear about any disgruntled, stressed-the-fuck-out teachers carrying out similar heinous acts. Even though, we're just as unstable, if not more.

We're *just* as capable.

A frequent day tremor has envisioned me whipping out a shotgun from the bottom drawer of my desk every time I'm asked a ridiculous question. That's all it would take, I fear, if I were crazy enough, if I were pushed over the edge of sanity toward the overwhelming abyss of lunacy.

"Mr. Cain, can I go to the bathroom?" *Boom.*

"Mr. Cain, what are we doing today?" *Boom.*

"Mr. Cain, is this going to be graded?" *Boom.*

"Mr. Cain, when are we ever going to use this?" *Boom.*

"Mr. Cain, why did you give me a C+…" *Boom. Boom. Boom.*

That's all it would take. Just one stupid question would turn my classroom into a lidless blender spouting crimson entrails all over the walls. If you value your life, never ask an unstable person a stupid question. Wait until after school, when the likelihood of the trigger being pulled diminishes exponentially.

Even a deranged English teacher hopped up on stupidity knows that 30>1. Nobody will lose sleep over one casualty. So why bother?

W hen the final bell rings to end the school day, most teachers attempt to get things accomplished for the next day. Not me. Especially not with two days left in the year. Normally, I just go into hiding to avoid having to deal with anyone. Minimal human contact is a necessity at the end of a day after having spent countless hours suffering from the unfortunate infestation of the student species around the building.

I teach *'Extreme Classroom Hibernation for the Unmotivated Teacher'* from 1:35 to 2:25 every day. Don't page me over the intercom. I won't come. Don't call me on my phone. I won't pick up. Don't knock on my door. I won't answer it. The only way to get in contact with me after school is by stalking my room and waiting patiently until I let my guard down in an attempt to exit the building.

Blanche Ellis knew this. Most ass-kissers are crafty when it comes to knowing everything about everyone else, and that's exactly how she knew what to do. She waited until there was movement and then pounced like a cheetah on a gazelle.

"Mr. Cain, so good to see you!" she exclaimed excitedly.

I let out a perturbed sigh and grudgingly replied, "Yes, Blanche? What is it?"

She seemed put off by my response but continued regardless, "It's Mrs. Ellis. I have an important message to deliver to you!"

"From who?"

"Mrs. Raker and the Administrative team of our glorious school."

"And what, pray tell, is their important message to me?" I insisted.

"Tomorrow at 2 o'clock, they are requesting a meeting with you."

"Is this mandatory or optional?"

Blanche stared directly into my irritable eyes, "I'm so glad that you asked. Well, I suppose that that is up to you."

"Well, what is this meeting about, if I may ask?" I inquired hesitantly.

"Your future, Mr. Cain. Mrs. Raker strongly urges you to attend."

"So then, mandatory? You could've just *said* that. No need to be all cryptic."

"Should I mark you down as confirmed then?" she asked with a bitchy undertone. I assumed she caught on to my overwhelming annoyance with her.

"Yes, Blanche. I suppose I'll be there."

Her face wrinkled into a mixture of insatiable abhorrence and smugness. She looked like a knock-off of Harvey Dent. One side of her face was the burnt to a crisp crotchety bitch who hated my guts, the other side the well-preserved, always smiling bitch, who also hated my guts but doesn't deliberately show it.

With an erratic grunt, Blanche stuck her nose high in the air, twisted away from my door and scurried down the hall to deliver my response to the deciders of my fate.

"Jackson! Oh, Jackson honey!"

For the love of God, what now? I thought as I rolled my eyes.

I turned around uneasily at first, for fear of seeing yet another person I'd prefer to avoid. But instead of a demon spawn, I saw the body of an angel rushing toward me and yelling out my name. It felt good to hear someone yelling my name in a positive manner for once.

"Ah Ms. Meadows, to what do I owe this pleasure?" I said in my finest attempt at chivalrousness.

"Darling, you're too sweet," she politely commented as she hugged me snuggly, "I wanted to ask you something. Would you like to meet me for dinner tonight? Strictly as friends, of course. You look a little down in the dumps today, Sugar, and I'd hate for that mood to carry over into tomorrow."

"That's very considerate of you Ms. Meadows," I declared softly, "but please forgive me as I'm not 100% certain if I will be able to take you up on that offer. You see, I have a girlfriend and I would feel very uncomfortable in such a compromising situation."

"I can understand that, dear. But as I said, it would be only as friends. I'm not really in the habit of breaking people up. If you change your mind," she handed me a piece of paper with an address and a time scrawled at the top of it, "that's where I'll be."

She kissed me delicately on the side of my right cheek and the sensation I felt when her soft lips pressed against my stubble was unlike anything I'd ever experienced. I've never felt that sensation before. Whenever Janice kissed me, it felt like nothing more than an unfortunate habit. Something she's expected to do, not necessarily something she wants to do. She doesn't put any passion behind it whatsoever. I felt more passion in a subtle kiss on the cheek from Darrah Meadows than I'd ever felt in a kiss anywhere on my body from Janice over the past year.

I watched her miraculous curves walk gracefully down the hallway and around the corner. Whenever Ms. Meadows walks, all the men stop and gaze. I followed her meticulously but remained at a distance so as not to be an obvious part of the pack of rabid horny male teachers hooting and howling at each robust movement of her body as she made her way promptly through the never-ending labyrinth of hallways and out the front doors.

There is never a greater feeling than busting through the front doors of the school building at day's end. For seven and a half hours every day I feel like a prisoner inside these walls. And I'm a teacher. You'd think I'd feel more like a prison guard as opposed to a lonely suicidal inmate. But no, that distinction is meant solely for the higher-ups. The Administration is the Warden, and the ass-kissing lackeys are the prison guards. Those of us just trying to get by one day at a time are no different than the students we attempt to teach. It's a prison to them, and it's a prison to us.

But as the sun beat down heavily upon my shoulders, I was able to feel the weight of yet another stressful day lifted and exposed of. At least, that is, until it would inevitably return the following morning when I step back into my shackles and complete my death row march back down the prison corridors to my cell in room 1287.

"See you tomorrow, you stupid fucker," Perry yelled affectionately from inside his Corvette before he screeched his tires along the pavement and bolted out of the parking lot and into the distance.

I walked swiftly to my '77 Camaro which was rusted over and looked like it had barely survived ample amounts of demolition derbies. My students, colleagues, and even my girlfriend constantly picked on me every waking moment about the piece of shit car I owned. But it was my car, and I loved it, regardless of what it looked like. I revved up the engine and was nearly ready to peel off school grounds much in the way Perry had but I noticed Bill Starks exiting the building with a couple other teachers and it prompted me to wait a second. I wanted to make sure he was doing okay. At face value, he looked better than he did during third block in the teacher's lounge, but as I recall he did inform me that he's an exceptionally gifted actor.

He passed by the passenger's side of my car and I quickly rolled down the window to offer a brisk word of farewell, "Have a good night Bill," I beckoned.

Bill noticed me in my seat only briefly and offered an abrupt nod of acknowledgement and continued on his way. The smile that he had plastered on his face while he walked with the others had seemingly disappeared instantaneously as the trio broke apart and each headed toward their respective vehicles.

I can only imagine what Bill has to go home to every night. It can't be much. An empty house and a bottle of whiskey is all he has to look forward to, which is nothing short of a damn shame. If I were in his shoes, I probably would've cowardly put a bullet in my brain by now.

I started to put my car in drive when I noticed at the far end of the school building a teacher with what appeared to be a couple of students, smoking. I pulled out of my spot slowly and as I approached the exit to the parking lot I could faintly see that it was Clark Wellers with one of my students, Demarcus, and another student I didn't quite recognize. The three were smoking together and Demarcus and the other student were inconspicuously handing Mr. Wellers what looked to be a wad of money.

As odd a situation as this appeared to be, I thought nothing of it at the time. After all Clark's a strange guy. He's fresh out of college, dresses like a hippie, and is not much older than half the students he teaches. How he even got hired looking as young as he does, I'll never know. Clearly he must have connections somewhere.

Why should I look deeper into things that obviously don't concern me? Hell, if it hadn't been for Mrs. Ellis stopping me as I was leaving my room, I wouldn't have even come across this apparent transaction between students and teacher in the first place. It's the Warden's fault. It's the prison guards fault. If they were doing their jobs and conducting a proper perimeter check, perhaps they'd take out Wellers with a couple of stray bullets to the chest that would make even Captain Hadley at Shawshank prison grin with delight.

The drive home is never an exciting ride. However, it's not necessarily dull either. An assortment of trees, a sprinkle of the slums, and an overabundance of open space envelopes the landscape of my commute like a tattered blanket covers a homeless man in the heart of Northern winters. It's a beautiful eyesore.

Stupid people have inherited the Earth and drive among us. And they all choose to overrun the roadways when *I'm* on them. They're everywhere and have even managed to assume the physical appearance of relatively normal people.

I can't remember the last time I drove home and didn't curse obscenities at other drivers. I generously hand out vulgarities like Oprah Winfrey hands out prizes to her studio audiences. If my grandmother were alive today, she'd fill my mouth with an entire bottle of liquid hand soap.

My apartment complex isn't anything to marvel at either. The Cordova is sub-standard compared to most of the communities that surround it. I wouldn't even be living in it if it weren't for Janice lighting a fire under my ass when we first started dating to get our own place together. I'd been in and out of the basements of high school friend's and old college roommates, living off table scraps from paycheck to paycheck. But when I met Janice that changed quickly. Before I knew it I had new friends, new priorities, and a new place to live. All it takes is one person to enter your life and change everything. And change everything she did.

I pushed open the door of the apartment and half-expected to see Janice doing her usual daily rounds of cleaning the place up while simultaneously bitching at me as I threw my bag to the floor. But the apartment was eerily quiet. I couldn't remember if she had work today or not, or any other prior commitments in which she needed to tend to, but typically if she's gone then she's doing something of dire importance.

The hours crept away silently and still there was no sign of Janice. I'd searched the apartment earlier to see if she'd left a note somewhere that I might have overlooked but was unable to find anything. At one point I had started to think that maybe she had pulled a stunt like Bill's wife and simply packed up and left. But I quickly tossed that out of my mind because I wasn't that lucky. Her names on the lease of the apartment and she wouldn't trust me to keep up with monthly rent payments if she ever left. Plus, all of her shit is still here. She values that stuff more than our relationship.

I don't think it would bother me if she were to ever leave though. She's changed my life. The jury's still out as to whether it's been a good change or a bad one. Life now feels too complicated. I've lost the simplicity I was used to; the simplicity that actually brought me some shred of joy.

Most people look to improve upon their past and move toward a brighter future. But my future looks bleak, the more it's spent with the people I concern myself with every day. I wake up to a miserable she-devil who hasn't even touched me in bed for over a month. I'm then greeted by Hitler reincarnated in female form the second I breeze into work. Then my primary interactions every day involve hopeless students, a pedophilic colleague, and a drunk mentor whose life is in shambles.

I just want to get back to where I was. I want my future to be my past. I just want to be happy again.

I sat somberly at the kitchen table munching on an apple from the bowl of fruit in front of me when I remembered that Darrah Meadows had invited me to dinner earlier today. Sure, I had respectfully declined, but she had kept the invitation open-ended in case I had a change of heart. The last thing I would ever want to do is twiddle my thumbs in an empty apartment and wonder when my girlfriend would come barging through our door. I started to empty my pockets for the piece of paper and read the address and time on it aloud to myself, *"51880 Brellington Tree Terrace, 8 pm."*

The road sounded familiar, but it wasn't one I traveled often as it was located in Downtown Coldbrook just outside of Obella Falls and that's where all the sketchy characters come out of the woodworks. Pimps and prostitutes, drug lords and drug addicts, and every type of gang affiliation known to man. It was scary enough driving that stretch of road during the daytime. It was a death wish to even consider making the trek at night.

Since Darrah had not said anything about picking her up for dinner, due to the uncertainty of my attending, I decided not to take the chance of driving there. As much as I hated the idea of it, the bus would ultimately have to do.

The Coldbrook city bus is no different than the Psychiatric Ward in your everyday hospital. There is never a shortage of crazies on the city bus. People with tics they can't control, people going through drug withdrawals and acting like they're possessed, people smelling of foul odors likely that of their own vomit, piss, and feces, and people who would suck you off for whatever you happened to have on you. I try to avoid the bus at all costs whenever I can, but I'd rather take my chances with public transportation into the ghetto than through my own means. For all I knew I could spend an hour eating dinner and come out to find my Camaro up on cinder blocks.

The ride to Brellington Tree Terrace went by smoother than I had anticipated it would. Not too many people on the bus for a Monday night, with the exception of an homeless black man in the back who kept muttering something about a "heartless wench," and an old lady who had plenty of empty seats to choose from, but elected to sit directly next to me and subsequently fall asleep drooling on my shoulder.

"Next stop, 51880 Brellington Tree Terrace," shouted the bus driver as the mountainous mass of steel came to a grinding halt.

I nudged the old lady off of my shoulder and pounced up to pay the remainder of my fare. As I started to walk off the last step of the bus I saw a flashing illuminated neon sign staring me square in the face, *Peepers*. A quick glance up and down the boulevard didn't clear matters up as it appeared that there weren't too many places to dine at on this stretch of the road. I was regrettably confused and thought that maybe the bus driver had dropped me off at the wrong location or that perhaps Darrah had given me the wrong address.

"This is 51880 Brellington Tree Terrace?" I implored frantically.

"Yessir, the best gentlemen's club in the city," he declared proudly. Clearly he was a regular.

"So, Ms. Meadows asked me to have dinner with her at a strip club?" I asked myself softly.

The bus driver had apparently thought that I was still addressing him and promptly responded, "Looks like it."

I shrugged it off, "Why would she want to have dinner at a strip club?"

Once again meant to be a rhetorical question, the bus driver spoke up, "I don't know and I don't care, pal. Now, could you please get the fuck off my step so that I can finish my nightly rounds?"

I threw the agitated driver an irate glance and jumped down off the final step and onto the curb looking around intently in an attempt to see if Darrah was anywhere in sight. I didn't see her or her car near the building or along the street. She could've gotten here in a similar fashion as me and could've already been in the building, as it was vastly approaching 8 o'clock.

I'd never been to a strip club before. I guess in a way that would make me a virgin of sorts. The only breasts I'd consistently seen over the past year have been Janice's and the ones in my Playboys under my mattress. I haven't the slightest clue as to what the etiquette is at a strip club or even what the environment would be like. I also didn't bring that much money with me either, so there likely wouldn't be any dollar bills being placed in anyone's G-string.

The bouncer at the front gate promptly asked me for my ID, which I provided him, and he motionlessly sent me in through the front corridor. My nostrils started to burn with the same sensual scent that I smelled so vividly on Darrah's body in the break room today. It was intoxicating. I felt like I was floating on air like a cartoon character struck with cupid's arrow toward the club's main opening, where all of the music was blaring at remarkably high decibels.

I made my way through the velvet curtain and saw a sight unlike any my eyes had ever beheld. Some of the most beautiful women from head-to-toe that I'd ever laid my eyes on were walking around topless asking patrons for private dances in the champagne lounge. Men were hooting and hollering and high-fiving each other and mindlessly throwing money at the many dancing bodies on the many different stages. It was a completely different world, unlike anything I knew existed. Unlike anything I was used to. For this was a world ruled solely by women, feeding off the perversion of men who could only think with their dicks and their wallets.

As pathetic as my own species looked, I could certainly understand exactly why they were under such exotic spells. All of these strippers were more than qualified to work there and had the ability to hypnotize you with every movement they made.

I walked up confidently to the bar where the bartender was wiping down the counter with precision.

"What are ya having, my man?" he blurted out before I could even get settled.

"I'll just have a beer. Any kind's fine," I yelled over the music as loudly as I could.

"Here ya go, partner," he barked and handed me a Corona.

"Thanks. You wouldn't happen to know if there's a Darrah Meadows here, would you?"

As fate would have it, he did. Apparently having heard this question numerous times before, the bartender pointed passed me without hesitation, directly at the main stage in the club. And there she was up on stage covered in nothing but glitter and high heels sensually frolicking around the stripper's pole like an acrobat at a Circus. She looked flawless.

I slowly made my way down the carpeted steps toward the main stage when the music started to fade which prompted Darrah to finish her routine and give up her place in the spotlight for the next stripper. As she walked down the side steps off the catwalk a bouncer placed a robe over her body. I waited casually near one of the open tables at the base of the main stage and she caught my eye as she walked passed me.

"I don't believe it, Jackson Cain, you came!" Darrah shrieked with joy, "Let's have a picture, shall we?"

Darrah pulled out her cell phone from the pocket of her robe. She grabbed ahold of my waist, lowered the top of her robe just enough to reveal her shoulders and bust, and kicked her right leg up behind her as she posed for the picture. As the flash lit up the room Darrah snuck in a quick peck on the side of my cheek.

"Ms. Meadows, it's once again a pleasure to see you," I said shrilly so as not to be drowned out by the music, "I can honestly say I'm shocked to see you like this!"

"Honey please, it's Darrah! Didn't think I had a wild side, did you?"

"No, I didn't. At least not one like this."

"Come with me, darling. Let's talk some place a little quieter. I can barely hear you over all of this noise."

She grabbed my hand and pulled me toward the champagne lounge near the back of the building. There was no music in this part of the club with the exception of the constant hum of the loud theatrics reverberating through the walls from the main room. Darrah led me to a smaller room located just off to the side of the lounge that had nothing in it but a red couch.

"Would you like something to drink?" she asked politely.

"No thanks, I already…" I began apologetically, before I realized that both of my hands were empty, "it appears I left my beer at the bar. I guess, I'll have to take you up on that offer."

"What would you like, sweetie?"

"Surprise me."

Darrah walked briskly toward the lonely bar just outside of the small room. She grabbed a bottle of Grey Goose and a small glass. She positioned her body in front of the bar, and I was unable to see her pour anything into the glass. It seemed odd. I could hardly focus on such a questionably erratic gesture anyway as I was more fixated on her body. She deliberately swayed her ass back and forth as if she were putting me in a sexual trance.

She came back with her finished alcoholic concoction, closing the curtain behind her and we sat down next to each other, with only a fraction of space between us as she handed me the glass. She was still in nothing but her robe and high heels, which made it extremely difficult for me to concentrate on anything she was saying. I could see her lips moving and I could faintly hear the sound of her voice elevating in tone as if she were asking me a question. I shook off the hypnotizing hormonal spell I had fell under and mumbled, "I'm sorry, what did you say?"

She chuckled at my obvious detachment from reality, "I asked you how long you've been here, silly."

"Oh, not long. Probably only like five minutes or so," I replied as I took a sip from my beverage.

It was unlike any glass of vodka I'd ever tasted. It was absolutely awful. It's probably a good thing Darrah excels at her exotic dancing because she's a terrible drink maker. She placed her hand underneath the glass and tipped it up, encouraging me to down it all.

"Oh, good. I'm so very happy that you decided to come."

I breathed heavily, still finding it hard to focus on anything but the curves underneath her robe that fit her body like a glove, "So am I. How uh, how long have you been doing this aside from teaching?"

She inched her body a little closer to mine, "Hm, I'd have to say it's close to about two years now. Sadly, I just don't earn enough as a teacher. I mean, you know what it's like. We're grossly underpaid. The state has basically driven me to pursue alternative options simply to make ends me."

Typically this was a topic I would have loved to have weighed my own opinions on, but my eyes were focusing entirely too much on Darrah's silky smooth skin far more than the topic of conversation. I could not care less about what she was saying at this particular moment.

"You uh, um," I stammered, "you looked really comfortable up on the stage. I mean, you truly have an amazing, athletic body."

"Awe, why thank you Jackson, that's so very sweet of you," Darrah responded softly as she leaned in and kissed me on the cheek.

"So, should we go get something to eat?" I blurted out, remembering only faintly that this whole endeavor was initially intended to be a dinner.

"What would you like to have, Sugar? I must admit, we have the finest desserts here," she answered as she perched her body up onto my lap and started to twirl her fingers around in my thick hair.

The way her fingers maneuvered around my scalp further heightened the hypnotic spell I was quickly falling under.

"What do you recommend, Darrah?" I mustered up the strength to ask.

She leaned forward and planted her luscious lips upon mine before making her way to my ear where she delicately whispered, "*Me.*"

Darrah slipped down off my lap and began doing a little striptease in order to discard the robe she was wearing. She was exhilaratingly beautiful. Her 5'5" exterior was slender and immaculately built proudly showing off a round, firm derrière and all too perfect breasts. She had intoxicating blood red lips and a button nose. Her silky smooth tan skin was accentuated by her bright blue eyes, and her long, bleach blonde hair. She could have easily been a supermodel or an actress of some sort. Why she chose to waste her miraculous God-given gifts by teaching witless high school students about economics and in her spare time stripping for grizzly perverts, I will never know.

She straddled her body upon my lap and began to unbuckle my belt as her lips made their way up my neck and to my lips. My hands were possessed. They had a mind of their own while she was working her magic, as they methodically stroked the small of her back before eventually settling with cupping the underside of her ass as it gyrated back and forth on my waist.

I dropped my head to her chest, holding her breasts to my lips, caressing them affectionately. I put my mouth over her right breast, flicking her nipple with my tongue.

Darrah moaned tenderly as I moved over to her left breast, fondling it and kissing it gently. Both of her hands were in my hair, gripping it tightly as she held my face to her breasts. Her quiet little gasps were music to my ears, and I found myself getting increasingly turned on with each passionate thrust of her pelvis on top of my body. I pushed myself up and moved my lips back to hers, and we began lustfully kissing again as our tongues hungrily danced with one another.

She grabbed the bottom of my shirt and pulled it up over my head as she lunged forward and we began kissing each other harshly like rabid wolves pouncing on their prey. Our bare skin pressed up against each other as she ran her fingers up and down my abs, brushing through my chest hair. My stiff cock pushed murderously against her body through my jeans. She rocked against it, sending tantalizing waves of pleasure throughout my entire body before she slipped down to the floor taking my unbuckled pants with her.

"Somebody's a little happy," she remarked about the size of my erection, as she looked up at me from her knees.

I couldn't even muster up the strength to utter a single word. There wasn't enough blood left in my brain to manifest a functional thought. All I could think about was this gorgeous creature merely inches away from putting me in her mouth. She was ready and so was I.

She wrapped her succulent mouth around my cock as she gingerly ran her tongue along the underside.

"Goddamn," I drawled as my power of speech momentarily returned. I groaned loudly as she continued to suck me off with her full, wet lips. I looked down, watching intently as her head went up and down like a wading boat lost on a stormy sea. I could feel my cock swell as the orgasm ferociously grew inside of me.

"Don't stop," I croaked, "oh, God, don't stop."

She didn't. She looked up at me with her seductive blue eyes and kept going, gripping my shaft with her hand and stroking it savagely as she sucked. I moaned violently as she brought me passed my breaking point. The pressure continued to build as she persisted with her flawless stroking and sucking, stroking and sucking. I couldn't hold back anymore. I was there. My cock exploded in her mouth, spraying my load down her throat. She didn't stop for a second, as she swallowed it all. She kept sucking and stroking, while spurt after spurt shot out of my cock and trickled down the edges of her pursed lips.

Darrah had released me of all my pent up emotion, all the anger, sadness, fear, and doubt. Every obnoxiously painful memory of the past year had ceased to exist for a few cheating seconds. And I felt free. She was like an intoxicating drug, that's for damn sure. In only a few minutes she had released me of all of my problems, all of my worries, if only for a moment, and I was thinking clearly for the first time in years. I felt euphoric. I felt elated. I felt at peace.

My head was pounding and finally I realized what I had just done.

"Oh, shit, shit, shit," I mumbled as I shot up from the couch and frantically yanked at my pants and re-buckled my belt, "shit."

Darrah's smile had suddenly vanished as she remained on her knees, "What? What's the matter?" she asked flabbergasted.

"I have a girlfriend. Oh, my God, oh no, I can't believe we did this. I can't believe *I* did this. Shit, fuck, shit."

"But didn't you enjoy it?" she inquired as a tear rolled down her beautiful face.

"I did, and that's exactly the problem," I admitted, "I'm in a relationship. I've never cheated on anyone in my life. I can't believe I just did this to Janice. I have to get out of here. I have to get home to my girlfriend. I have to go. I'm sorry."

I looked at Darrah with a mixed emotion of gratitude and displaced sadness as she continued to tear up. She managed to muster up the courage to speak as I made my way toward the exit of the champagne lounge, "I swear to God, if you walk out that door, Jackson, you'll never get to have me again," she shouted as I brushed aside the curtain and lunged for the exit, "I can make your life a living hell, I promise you!"

She continued her screams of displeasure as they echoed throughout the club. As I made my way passed the bouncer's and out the front door her voice started to trail off and finally muffled as my feet hit the concrete outside.

I had no idea where to go. I wasn't that familiar with the city. There's bus stops on nearly every corner downtown, but at this time of night, the last thing I wanted to do was stay in one place for fear that that might make me an easy target for crazies. I walked with a brisk stride down Brellington Tree Terrace toward the south side of Coldbrook. I had heard stories, mostly through my students who lived in this area, that you were less likely to get shot on the south side. So I was hoping those myths were accurate. My life was in the hands of their street knowledge. God help me.

With my head bent forward and my hands buried deep in my pockets I came across an almost deserted intersection about six blocks from the strip club with only one flickering street lamp. I'm pretty sure this is where most horror stories originate. How fortunate of me to find it, as I subconsciously started thinking of the theme music to *A Nightmare on Elm Street*. Perfect.

This may not be the place I want to be, I thought.

I kept my head low and tried to walk as quickly as possible toward the next corner where the street lights were at least functioning properly when I heard some muffled noises down an alleyway to my right. Now they say that curiosity killed the cat. Well, it would likely be my killer too, as I stopped dead in my tracks in an attempt to see what the commotion was. This is exactly how people seal their fate in slasher films. But what if somebody was getting mugged? Or even worse hurt? I'm not sure I could live with myself if I saw it happening and simply let it go.

I took very precise baby steps toward the darkened alley as the muffled moans were getting louder. I couldn't quite make out the tone of the moans, but it made me feel uneasy, so I anticipated the worst.

"H-hello? Is there anyone down there?" I shouted and listened as my voice echoed between the walls.

I heard a faint murmur and a frantic rustle of bodies behind a set of dumpsters midway down the alley which startled me.

"Who the fuck are you's?" came a low voice from within the shadows, "You's a coppa? What are you's doin' here?"

"I'm, I'm not a cop. Just a lost guy looking for the bus. I was walking by and heard a noise and thought maybe somebody was in trouble."

A middle-aged black man walked out of the shadows, tripping over his own feet as he was desperately trying to buckle up his pants. I looked passed his mountainous frame and caught a tired glimpse of a young black girl who looked as if she were not much older than the students I teach sobbing loudly as she fumbled at pulling up her underwear.

"The only one who might be in trouble, is you's," he declared pointedly as he got closer to me.

I was shaken, yet surprisingly calm given the circumstances, "Oh no, no trouble, I insist."

The man sized me up with his eyes and after only a few moments must have realized that physically I was of no threat to him. He started to make his way toward the corner when the young girl spoke up, "Wait, where my money is?"

"What money, you's thievin' skank! Get on outta here!"

"It's fifty for a throw! I want my money!"

"Go home girl!" he squealed as he tossed a crumpled up ten dollar bill on the ground, "You's wasn't even that good!"

I stood in awe as I watched the defeated girl saunter toward the wad of money on the ground. She looked like she just went 15 rounds with Mike

Tyson. She was likely battered and bruised in more ways than one. I didn't know what to say. I wasn't even sure as to what I just witnessed. Either she was raped. Or she was a young prostitute.

"Are you okay?" I asked superficially.

She picked up the ten dollar bill, examined it, and placed it inside her bra, "I's fine. You's cost me forty dollars, y'know. He just started."

I was surprised by her response, "Oh. My apologies."

"Don't worry 'bout it. You's wanna have a go?" she asked hungrily.

"Um, no. I don't. I think that we both should get home."

"Home? Psh, it's still early and I's gots money to make. What are you's gay? You's don't like whatchu see?"

She stepped toward me and I could scarcely make out more of her facial and bodily features under the flickering street lamp. She looked familiar, but I couldn't quite pinpoint where I'd seen her before. Her bruises were old and were scattered on her arms, legs, and even her neck. With the exception of a few unsightly scars and a black eye, she was a very beautiful girl.

"No, I'm not gay. But you are right about one thing. I don't like what I see," I said to her in a fatherly tone, "why are you doing this to yourself?"

"Look mister, I's ain't got much of a home life, aight? Ma family can't afford nuttin. So, I's gotta do dis, for them. Now, get to steppin' if you ain't gonna be a payin' customer," she said sourly as she stepped even closer to me, when suddenly her mouth dropped open as if she'd just seen a long lost relative, "oh ma God, Mr. Cain?"

"How do you know my," I started, and then I finally got a good look at the detail in the curves and terrain of her battered face, "Daneesha? Is that you?"

She was one of my favorite students from my first year of teaching, back when I actually cared about what I did and who I taught. I remember thinking then when I first met her that she would be going places. Of all the people in her fourth period class, she would be the one to make it out, to make the best out of a bad situation. But after she moved on to the next grade, I saw less and less of her, and eventually none of her. Now look at her. She's still got a hint of her physical beauty, but it's all masked by an unfortunate life of prostitution. All that hope and promise that was locked away inside her and ready to burst two years ago, was completely gone.

Usually my predictions about my students' futures were right on the money, but this one was a terrible swing and a miss.

"Yes, Mr. Cain. It's me," she remarked somberly.

"What in the world has happened to you?" I asked as my voice cracked.

I hadn't seen many of the students from my first year of teaching in a long time because they'd all either dropped out of school or graduated. To finally see one was heartbreaking. Especially one who was supposed to be a shining example of how you can grow up in the worst kind of conditions and still make something of yourself. She'd taken fifty steps backward from where she was on the path to being.

"I'm out on the streets tryna make a living. I gotta eat somehow, Mr. Cain."

God's not supposed to let this kind of shit happen. Good people, full of promise and potential, aren't supposed to be dealt a shitty hand draw after draw. If you keep getting low cards, eventually you'll fold.

I've been angry at God before, but never like this. The passion I had been losing was beginning to resurface, if just for a split second, "But how did it happen? I mean, you of all people. You had so much drive and determination when I had you. Where did it go? Where did the Daneesha I had two years ago go?"

"She gone, Mr. Cain. And she ain't comin' back. Ma daddy left. Ma momma lost the house. And now we's livin' on what we's can scrape togetha out in da real world. Ma momma told me, ain't no man lookin' for a woman with anything to offer other than what she can do in tha bedroom. So I's do dis to get a little money. We's can't afford no college, so I's didn't go. We's out in tha streets, forced to live in the here and now, Mr. Cain. People in ma neighborhood, they's don't get out. There's no gettin' away. They's stay right where they is, and that's that. Why should I's think any different?"

I couldn't believe what I was hearing. Daneesha never used to approach life with such a helpless attitude. She was resigned to her fate. Her mother's fate. It didn't make sense that she should have to suffer because her mother didn't have the drive inside of her to get out. She was born in a prison cell and knew no other life.

"I don't know what to say," I admitted to her.

"You's don't gotta say nuttin' Mr. Cain. I's fine with where I's is. Just go on home. This ain't no place for someone like you's to be," she said as her eyes tore deep gashes into my heart.

I reluctantly nodded my head and gave her a quick hug. Before letting her go, I pulled out my wallet and gave her what little money I had on me and watched as she gave me a painful smile.

It's tough to watch the ones you care about breaking apart piece by piece in front of you. It's even tougher knowing you can't do a damn thing to stop it from happening. Sometimes all you can do is just watch them crumble.

I made it to the corner of Vero Boulevard and Silverline Lane and stopped at the bus stop bench. I started to regret not bringing my Camaro. I could have been home already. Instead I'm in the middle of a dilapidated city I'm unfamiliar with late at night, twenty dollars poorer, with a throbbing head.

Better start writing my obituary now. It's only a matter of time before my mangled body is found on the side of the road and I make national headlines for stupidly being in a sketchy place at a time of night that even police deliberately try to avoid.

The wait for the city bus is like an extreme test of endurance. It compares in magnitude to the saturation chamber meant to treat schizophrenia eccentric millionaire Steven Price was thrown into in *House on Haunted Hill.* Every second wasted I can feel my sanity fleeting from my mind. When you're alone, paranoia sets in. You see things that aren't there. And you think things that are there are simply hallucinations.

I tried to close my eyes and envision that I was somewhere else entirely. When I was younger my father would always tell me that if I closed my eyes and truly focused on what I wanted and whispered it aloud to myself, God would hear it and it would appear in front of me. At that time I usually only wanted something simple like a Popsicle, which my father would sneakily place in front of me before I re-opened my eyes. It was a clever little trick that worked for years until I got older and started to ask for unrealistic things. That was when my father broke the news to me that life doesn't work that way, and that God doesn't actually listen to us.

It had been years since I thought of my father. But when I closed my eyes, it made me think of him.

"Please bring me the city bus," I whispered to myself with my eyes still closed.

"Who you's talkin' to man?" came a high-pitched voice that startled me out of my seat.

I opened my eyes and saw an emaciated black man with a cane gingerly strolling up to the bench as a pair of headlights gleamed in the distance.

"Um, nobody. Just myself, I guess."

"Well, which is it? Nobody or yourself?" he asked.

"Myself," I chuckled slyly, as he responded in the way I would if I were dealing with an indecisive student.

"Well, cut that shit out, people will thinks you's crazy," he declared sharply.

"What if I am?" I asked him stoically.

He laughed, "Then you's gonna fit in just fine in dis part of town. Keep actin' like that and nobody will cross you's."

The bus pulled up mystically through the evening haze. I got up from my spot on the bench and approached the doors.

"You coming?" I asked the stranger on the bench.

"Nah, I's don't go on the bus. Too many crazies take the bus."

I flashed a quiet smile and thought to myself, *I think he might literally be crazy. But if he's crazy, what's that make the people on the bus that* he *thinks are out of their minds?*

"Where to partner?" quizzed the bus driver.

"Cordova Apartments, Obella Falls," I responded as I handed him the fare.

"Okay, grab a seat. Couple of stops before I head out that way, so sit tight," he said as the bus instantly started to roll down the pavement like an avalanche.

There were more bodies on the bus than I anticipated there would be at this time of night. I grabbed a seat near the middle of the bus just a few empty seats shy of a skinny white woman in a ratty tank top. I tried my best to avoid making eye contact with her, but every tic and twitch she made took me by surprise and I couldn't help but glance over to see if she was all right.

She got up and moved a seat closer to me, "You like what you see, papi?"

"No," I said firmly as I leaned away from her.

"Come on, I saw you looking at me. You want a taste? I'll give you a taste for a good price."

"Look, miss. I'm just trying to get home, and God willing I'd like to get there with as little interaction with other people as possible. So if you don't mind," I shooed her away in the way someone might shoo away an animal they don't particularly like, and moved to the open seat adjacent to me.

The next thing I knew she was back in the seat next to me grabbing ahold of my arm and my shirt as she started to yell, "Help! Somebody! He's trying to rape me! Help me! Please, make him stop!"

I jerked my arm away from her and watched her fall to the floor of the bus in a hysterical rage, crying her eyes out as the mascara ran down her face.

"What the fuck is wrong with you?" I asked her in a menacingly low tone.

She continued to wail away until she realized that nobody was coming to her rescue, so she promptly hopped to her feet and went back into the seat she had just fallen from. There were no knights in shining armor ready to save the life of a 98-pound drug addict on this bus. Clearly she was either a regular to this bus and everyone knew all of her quirks except me, or nobody cared. She resumed her periodical twitches, and threw an angry glare my direction every few minutes.

After a while we reached a stop just outside of Coldbrook. A few of the passenger's in the back of the bus got off and so did the crazy crack whore across from me. Before the bus driver could pull away a man rushed over from the other side of the street and rapped on the side of the bus to catch his attention. A young man, probably no more than a few years older than me skipped up the steps and gave the driver an address, thanking him politely for letting him on.

With more seats to choose from than earlier, I expected the man to sit right next to me like most of the crazies seem to do. But he didn't. He took a seat two seats down, across from me. He crossed his legs and pulled out a small book from his arm bag and began reading silently to himself. It vaguely resembled a bible, but didn't quite look like any bible I'd ever seen. The fancy script on the front cover was worn out and faded, making it impossible to decipher.

I wanted to stick to my guns and just remain quiet the rest of the ride home. But this person actually seemed normal. And he was reading. As an English teacher, I don't see that happening a whole lot, so it intrigued me enough to speak up.

"What're you reading there?" I pried.

"Oh, this old thing? It's not actually a book. Just a journal," he replied.

"Oh okay. I'm sorry for interrupting you. I'm a teacher and I was just shocked to see somebody actually carrying around something to read."

He chuckled, "Yeah, I hear you there. Books are pretty much being replaced. It's all electronic now."

"I know. Faces are either buried in a smart phone or some kind of tablet. Only time I ever see books are in my classroom or at a bookstore."

"You ain't kidding. And I'll never understand it either," he lifted his head entirely from his journal and looked at me, "the whole reason I enjoy buying books, is to actually feel them in my hands, and to smell the hard work in between the pages. There's nothing that compares to that new book smell."

"I know exactly what you mean," I agreed wholeheartedly, "I've tried to convince my students of this numerous times but they just shrug it off and go right back to typing away their grammatically incorrect text messages on their phones."

"It's such a shame. Sounds like we have a new generation of idiots primed to come out of the schools soon."

I laughed. Probably louder than I should have. He was right after all, "We certainly do."

The man closed his book, got up from his seat and approached the seat next to me. There wasn't much to him. Narrow build with thinning brown hair on top of his head and scruffy facial hair aligning the walls of his jaw. He adorned a blue suede vest with what appeared to be a velvety grey church symbol up near his left shoulder. But upon closer inspection it couldn't have been a church symbol. And if it was, it was no church I'd ever seen or heard of before. This was not necessarily someone I would approach under normal circumstances, but compared to the rest of the people I'd encountered tonight, he was the only one I felt at ease with.

I caught a quick glimpse of the bus driver who kept frantically looking up at his rearview mirror with worry, always diligent and interested in what's happening in front of him as well as behind him.

"The name's Carter. Carter Corrish," he asserted as he tossed a hand toward me.

I froze at the sound of his name. I couldn't quite put my finger on it, but the man's name sounded eerily familiar to me. I shrug it off and smiled.

"Jackson Cain," I responded in kind, "So what kind of stuff are you scribbling in your journal there? Are you a writer?"

"Not in the conventional sense."

"What do you mean by that?"

"I write, but I don't write for monetary gain," he exclaimed, "I write down my thoughts and feelings toward the world we live in. I consider myself more of a poet. A life poet, if you will."

My smile instantly erased and my intrigue in what this man had to say started to diminish, "Oh, you're one of those people? What do they call them? Hermits. So what religion or lifestyle are *you* pushing?"

"I'm not pushing any kind of religion. In fact, I'm pushing the opposite. I'm pushing life, my friend, nothing more, nothing less. New hope. New beginnings. That's what I'm pushing for. I'm apathetic about all manner of things and find it hard to believe a deity exists."

"Can I ask why?"

"Yes, you can! Truthfully, I wish more people would ask that! Then maybe there would be more people willing to accept the impracticality of stressing over beliefs and just live life. I saw the light, as soon as I acknowledged the undeniable likelihood of there being no God controlling our fate but instead our own actions controlling our fate, life began to make a lot more sense, my friend."

"That's a pretty bold stretch there, Carter. I mean, how can you convince people who believe in the doctrines of their religion that God doesn't exist?"

"It's simple. How can one believe in something they've never seen?"

"That's not how faith works," I assured him, "people kill each other and are willing to die over what they believe in."

"Which you can't deny is stupid. What are your beliefs, sir?"

"I have no beliefs," I started and I could faintly see his eyes start to swell with pride and his mouth widen with pleasure, "I don't pretend to dwell on anything. People are free to live and die and breathe and pray any way they please. As long as they aren't directly affecting me and my way of life, why should I care what their beliefs are?"

He looked a little put off by my response, "But you didn't really answer my question though. What do you believe in?"

"I don't think it matters what I believe. I'm convinced that there's a Heaven and a Hell. Whether there are angels and demons roaming around each, I don't know. I'd like to think there are, but I can't be sure. Nobody can be. I really can't say definitively whether I believe in a single God or not. Some days I don't think there is, because if there was a lot of the senseless shit that happens in this world doesn't really paint Him in a positive light. Other days, I get to witness a miracle or two in life and find it hard to believe that we're all here by accident. There's something out there that's far beyond our understanding. We just gotta have faith that if there is a spirit out there looking down on us that one day, if we're lucky, maybe we'll get to meet them."

"Spoken like every other person I've met on my travels. I just can't swallow that garbage. I refuse to believe anything I can't see with the naked eye."

I was shocked to learn that someone could be so hardheaded and so openly disregard what I thought or what others thought. He was convinced he was right. His truth was the only truth there was. Everyone else was wrong. He didn't care about anything or anyone, other than himself. But I guess I can't fault him for how passionately he feels about life. Maybe he had the right idea. After all he looked a hell of a lot more at peace with life than me. Here I worry every day whether or not I'm destined for Heaven or Hell. Most days it's the latter. Maybe I shouldn't care what happens to me. In life or the afterlife.

But if you don't have even a shred of faith in fate and the things you can't control, what kind of a life are you living? I already knew the answer: *a care free one.*

"And I respect that, truly I do," I said softly trying not to reveal that I was actually lying as I brought my hand up to ease my throbbing head, "it's a pretty outrageous outlook you have there, but if that's what you believe, then I respect it."

"Thank you," he responded and got up from his seat as he noticed the bus driver was about to stop at his destination, "looks like this is my stop. I've never been in this part of town before; I hope it's not as sketchy as the last one was. It was nice to see you again, Jackson."

My mind had glossed right over what he had said as I watched him bury his book back into his hand bag and leap off the bus into the night, without the slightest bit of faith in anything that might shield him from harm.

"Next stop, Obella Falls, fella," shouted the bus driver.

With the commotion settled down and the bus eerily empty, I leaned my head back against the fogged up window to rest my eyes. I couldn't help but think about the conversation I'd just had and realized that I've slowly been turning into Carter Corrish over the past year in my lack of caring about anything other than myself. I just wish I could approach life and living like he does.

I arrived at Cordova just shy of midnight. The apartment was quiet. Not a single sound emanated from within. Janice must have been sound asleep. I crept in like a burglar trying not to give any indication that I was there. I made my way into the bedroom, easing the door open slowly, and was startled by what I saw, an empty bed.

No sign of Janice. Just an empty room, exactly the way it was when I left it earlier. She still hadn't been home yet.

For the moment, it looked like my crazy night out would go unnoticed. I wouldn't need to explain myself or get involved in some pointless lecture as to why I need to let Janice know where I am at all times because that's what good partners do. If only she followed her own damn rules once in a while.

I hopped into bed with half of my clothes still on, too tired to even be bothered with the energy required to take them off. What a day from Hell this has been.

If only I'd instantly fall asleep the minute my face grazes the side of the pillow. Sleep doesn't come easy, however, especially for a teacher.

Good teachers will lie in bed and worry about every meticulous component of what they have planned for the next day. And their brain will throw them scenario after scenario for them to overanalyze and misinterpret causing them to forget to sleep. It's a never-ending cycle that goes on all year long.

Bad teachers will lay in bed and envision scenario after scenario of their students spontaneously bursting into flames or the school building blowing up and leaving nothing but piles of rubble, preferably with everyone they hate trapped somewhere inside. Oh, the satisfaction they would feel driving to work the next day just to hear that school would forever be canceled.

Unfortunately, things never go the way you want them to.

I usually just glare out my bedroom window at the night sky and think about all of the things I could be doing instead of teaching. I could be an artist, a poet, an author; all of them top my list. But how could anyone live off such careers? Most of the people who broke boundaries and paved the roads for future generations didn't see a cent while they were alive. Their true genius was realized long after they were dead and gone. Most of us don't get to live for even a split second in glory. We'll paint, we'll rhyme, and we'll write our lives away, pushing our brittle fingers to the bone, just to fade into relative obscurity leaving whatever masterpieces we made while we were in our flesh behind.

When I die, whatever I produced while I was alive will be buried with me. If no one could cherish it while I was breathing, I don't want anyone to waste his or her breath on it when I'm gone.

I thought about Janice, too. For the first time in a couple of months, I actually missed her. Once you get used to having a body beside you in bed, it doesn't feel right when it's empty. But lately, even when she's been here, she hasn't actually *been here.* It's more like I have a ghost lying beside me, rather than a lover. Physically her body is there, but emotionally and spiritually, she's somewhere else entirely. It's not tough to pick up on the subtle hints the person you sleep with is sending you that they want to be somewhere else.

I just wish I knew where she wanted to be. Hell, maybe that's where she was now.

I fell out of the sky for miles around four in the morning and crashed angrily on top of my desk in my classroom. It was disturbingly quiet, as the hallways were dark and the picturesque wide open valleys that were typically right outside my window were nothing more than a paltry extension of the starless night sky. There was no color anywhere, with the exception of the velvety blue lettering on my high school alma mater shirt.

Where is everybody? I thought, as I glanced up at the clock which was rapidly ticking away the hours. The hour hand circulated expeditiously to the point where it appeared it might fly off its hinges.

Bodies entered through the door and weaved in and out of the desks in the room, moving as hurriedly as the clock on the wall. The calendar at the front of the room started spitting out sheet after sheet for each passing day.

Nobody stopped. Nobody slowed down. It was a never-ending race against time. I gazed over at the teacher's desk and saw myself sitting there aging along with the clock on the wall. I was going from having hair to gray hair to no hair, gaining weight as I was gaining years. My expression never changed. There was no smile, no reaction, not a single emotion emitted. There wasn't even a mouth after a while. Every time I blinked there were less and less features on my aging face. No nose, no eyes, no eyebrows, just a blank visage from an expressionless man.

There I was just wilting away. The passion and desire within me growing smaller and smaller with every passing minute. I looked out the classroom window and saw a glorious sunrise on the horizon that harbored my innermost dreams. There they sat perched in the distance, seemingly an arm length away. But I couldn't reach them. My feet were weighted down to the ground and I was sinking through the floorboards like quicksand.

My now old and feeble expressionless counterpart got up from his place behind the desk as if to help me out of the floor, but he didn't. A Cheshire cat-like grin appeared on the empty face, as he began a verbal onslaught of continuous laughter. A robin flew onto the shoulder of my faceless counterpart, watched me struggle in agony for a moment, and then flew away.

The entire room slowed down from its torrent of movement and a crowd of expressionless bodies added to the deafening laughter. The laughter continued to grow and grow and so did my head as I continued to sink deeper and deeper into the floorboards. But before my head could explode, I disappeared.

My alarm clock roared viciously, jolting my body frenziedly into consciousness. The whole morning routine seemed like a blur. It's the same thing every day. Every minute detail is done exactly the same every day. Mentally I don't even have to be awake for it, as my body knows specifically what to do. Bathroom, shower, dress, breakfast, bathroom, and out the door. Occasionally a kiss goodbye to the sleeping ghost still in bed gets sprinkled into the routine, but not this morning as she was still missing in action.

My body remained on autopilot all the way to the school. A cup of coffee and obnoxiously loud music normally does the trick in waking me up, but caffeine had no effect and my ears were immune to the noise today.

The line to get into the building in the morning is nothing short of dreary. Teacher after teacher looking as if they were nothing more than rotting corpses. Just emotionless bodies falling into Pink Floyd's meat grinder. Flashing any kind of smile at this assembly line could very easily set in motion the beginning of the apocalypse. Apparently, I'm not the only one already looking forward to this day being over.

I scribbled my signature next to my name on the clipboard to ensure yet another day of being paid and my worst nightmare was painstakingly guarding the office door.

"Don't forget, you've got a very important meeting to attend this afternoon, Jackson. Don't be late," Mrs. Raker snipped at me with a smug smile.

Oh, how I would love to rip that fucking smirk off her irritating face.

"I wouldn't dream of it, Jasmine," I replied slyly.

She shrugged off my obvious attempt at disrespect by using her first name and with a flick of the hair and a roll of the eyes she made her way towards the mail room at the end of the office hallways. Seeing the direction in which she was going, I elected not to check my mail for fear of running into even more people I'd rather avoid and instead made a quick getaway into the main lobby. But when you deliberately try to avoid one person, you always find another.

And goddamn, she looked incredible today. Darrah looked like she should be on the runway giving away Victoria's secret. But that's never going to happen again. It shouldn't have even happened the first time. I found out firsthand exactly why men shouldn't think with their dick. It only gets us into trouble.

One look at me and she'd probably try to hang me from the rafters by my testicles. She started to make her way toward my direction and faintly made eye contact with me, but like a coward I bolted through a front set of doors and up the stairwell, taking an alternate route toward my classroom.

T he last couple days of school, I usually move like a zombie and not the genetically altered, super-fast ones that you can't escape from. I'm talking about the eerily slow, *Night of the Living Dead* type zombies.

I'm far less motivated than I am at the beginning of the year, and the hours just seem to drag continuously. Locking me in a room full of annoying students, who also notice how slow the time is moving, makes it move even more laggardly. Every class period my only objective becomes to deflect any and all comments that reference the speed of the clock with ninja-like precision.

The first two periods felt like I was slowly drowning in an hourglass, with sand pelting me on the head every few seconds. Yet, it was taking forever for me to suffocate under the weight of the sand. All I wanted it to do was explode at full force and drown me and relieve me of my suffering.

"Mr. Cain," a low voice acknowledged me as I sat reclined behind my desk with a newspaper over my face, "yo, Mr. Cain."

I removed the newspaper and glanced up at the clock on the wall which whispered to me that there was only five minutes left of class. I took my feet off my desk and saw Demarcus standing near me with his Final Exam review packet in his hands.

"Just set it right there on the corner of my desk, Demarcus," I remarked.

"Mr. Cain," he started again.

I interrupted him, "Just right there," I reiterated as I pointed.

"Yeah, no shit," he said which caught my attention, "was that you I saw yesterday after school in the Camaro?"

"Probably was. I don't believe anyone else has the same kind of car as me."

"That's a sweet ride, dawg," he complimented me as he smacked my hand and gave me a fist bump like some ritualistic handshake we'd never practiced.

"What were you doing behind the staircases next to the auditorium?" I asked him, knowing I probably wouldn't get a straight answer, "Looked like you were with a couple of other guys."

"Yeah, I was. We was smoking."

"You know you're not supposed to smoke on school grounds. If you're inside the fence, you're technically on school grounds. Was that all you were doing?"

He started to fidget a little bit and looked increasingly uncomfortable each time I pried a little further.

"No, just smoking. That's all," he answered and tried to walk away, but I grabbed his arm.

"Are you sure that was it? I saw you give somebody a wad of cash. What was that for?" I inquired.

I noticed a bead of sweat starting to trickle down the side of his face, "No. It was nothing. I mean, there wasn't any money. I don't know what you're talking about."

He fumbled over his words, so I pressed him further, "Why was Mr. Wellers there?" I asked.

"Look man, it's none of your damn business, aight? Just squash it," Demarcus snapped as the bell sounded to mark the end of the period and every person jumped out of their seats and filed out of the room toward the cafeteria.

Something fishy is going on there, I can feel it, I thought.

Not even five minutes of my lunch period had passed when I received a knock on my door. I often try my damnedest to elude the presence of others throughout each day, especially during lunch which is my lone moment of tranquility on my days without a planning period, but I regrettably made eye contact with the silhouette in my window so I felt obligated to see who it was. To my surprise it was Clark Wellers.

"Mr. Cain, so nice to see you. Would it be all right if I come in for a moment?" he asked sheepishly.

"Of course, of course, by all means. Make yourself at home."

Perhaps I shouldn't have been so cordial, as he made himself comfortable at my desk by promptly sitting down in my chair.

"I got a visit from Demarcus just a few minutes ago," he started as I sat on top of one my student's desks and folded my arms feigning interest, "he told me you were asking him a lot of questions."

"That's right. I told him that I saw him smoking after school yesterday just outside of the building."

"And that was all you saw?" Clark interrogated.

"As a matter of fact, it wasn't. There were two other individuals there with him."

I could see the wheels ferociously turning in Clark's mind as his dark green eyes peered into my soul, "Did you happen to get a good look at who they were? Or what else they were doing?"

"I'm going to cut to the chase here Clark, I saw you, Demarcus, and another kid I've never seen before out there smoking yesterday. And that's all whatever, I could honestly care less about that, that's your business. But I saw Demarcus hand you money. That's what I'm curious about. That's what's got me prying," I asserted.

Clark brought his hands up to his face and continued to stare into a world invisible to the naked eye, "You want in, is that what you're saying?"

"In on what?" I asked, confused.

Clark let out an enormous sigh and brushed back the locks of his flowing black hair from his face, "I make out pretty well."

"What are you talking about?"

"Demarcus and Alberto are my top guys."

"Clark, you're going to have to enlighten me here. I still don't follow."

He looked agitated that he had to keep explaining further, as he glanced around the room and got up to peer out the window of the door to make sure nobody was around to overhear him.

"You ever hear of drug trafficking?" he asked in almost a muted whisper.

"Can't say that I have."

"Jesus, how old *are* you? You act like you're a fucking hundred. I'm the manufacturer, and those two are my suppliers," he stopped and checked the doorway again, "I give 'em the goods, and they sell 'em to the kids in the school. It's a sweet gig. I make a shit ton of extra money this way. I'm talking an additional 5 to 7k a month."

"So you're doping these kids up on drugs and cashing in on it?"

"C'mon Jackson, I don't get caught up in making sure these kids are in good health. They ain't my kids. I give 'em the high they want and they get hooked. It's no hard feelings, but it gives me a much heavier pocket, if you know I'm saying."

I rolled my eyes, "What are you giving them?"

"It's my own special concoction I stumbled across in college, a potent mixture of LSD, Valium, and Ritalin. I call 'em blasters."

"How long have you been doing this?"

"Just started the idea this year. Snooped out a couple of guy students I felt I could trust and wanted to see if they were looking for some money to earn, and business has been booming since I reeled them in. I figure a few more years of this, and I'll have more than enough money saved in the bank to retire early," he said as his grin widened.

"And the students," I inquired, "do they know who their manufacturer is?"

"Nope. They only know me as the Kingpin. I keep a pretty tight wrap on making sure that no one figures out that it's me. Only people that know I'm the Kingpin are Demarcus, Alberto, and now you," he remarked as he was once again sizing me up with his eyes, "I'm thinking we could call you the Chief. You won't make as much as I do, but I'll cut you a decent slice of the pie every month. You'll be far better off than you are right now financially, I'm sure. I mean, I've seen what you drive."

I couldn't believe the audacity of this man. And not even just him. First Perry and now Clark. One has a stacked black book of female students to pimp out to anyone who looks sexually frustrated and the other heads a school wide drug trafficking ring, all the while right under the noses of administration. And they both are trying to recruit me into their potentially career ending and life ruining schemes.

Every day I feel more and more like I'm the only sane person still residing within the walls of this building. And even *I* was far from rational.

"So how 'bout it, *Chief?*" Clark asked with an outstretched arm.

"I don't know," I started as Clark began to retreat his hand as he apparently felt betrayed that I didn't jump for joy and gravel at his feet while calling him Kingpin, "I'm probably not the best person to recruit for your little operation."

"And why is that? I've already told you about it, and I'm not about to just throw information like that out there to someone who isn't going to be a part of it. How am I supposed to know you won't leave this room and report it to Cpl. Dayton downstairs?" he quizzed me stoically.

"I guess you've got a point, I haven't really given you any confidence that I would keep this a secret. However, I haven't given you any indication that I wouldn't either," I said firmly as Clark looked momentarily intrigued and far less antsy than he was a second ago, "I wouldn't be a great fit because administration has been barking up my tree nonstop the past few days. If this were on my plate too, it'd only be a matter of time before they sniffed it out and we all go down."

I'm a pretty good liar when the moment calls for it. And sadly, that wasn't entirely a lie. On the one hand, I didn't want anything to do with Clark's little drug trafficking operation which I was positive would inevitably be found out at some point, but on the other hand administration has been watching my every move so if I *were* willing to join it, they'd be on my ass faster than my eventual cellmates would be.

I could see an immense flourish of gratitude wash over Clark's face. Clearly he saw my admittance of always being watched by administration as the decisive cue that he could trust me not to tell anyone his secret for fear of both of us losing our jobs.

He extended his arm again for a handshake and slapped the back of my shoulder gently,

"Appreciate you informing me of that. Could have been bad for us. Just remember, the offer is always on the table Chief. If things cool down with the administration, that is."

And with that offer left floating in the air, Clark pushed open my door and bolted down the hallway leaving me a mere three minutes to eat lunch.

Every school day should end directly after lunch. Nothing gets accomplished after lunch. Especially at the end of the year. The second half of the school day sees teachers fizzle out and shrivel up, while students become more energetic and focus less. It goes from a smooth running classroom in the morning to a dysfunctional zoo in the afternoon simply because of the exploits of lunch.

All I want is to go home and be somewhere where my mood is marginally less likely to be affected by obnoxious people, both students and staff.

As the clock recklessly counted down each meaningless minute of the last period of the day, I crazily thought I'd be able to coast through the remaining seconds just snoring heavily at my desk but my students would have none of it. A small minority of students insist that you teach them something every day, regardless if it's review time or not. They don't care if it's something small or gigantic, trivial or important, pointless or brilliant. They simply want to force you to plant one new seed of knowledge in their puny little brains. I guess I can't fault them for *caring*, when too few people do. Especially me.

"Mr. Cain, since it's our last day together," inquired Laila, one of my brightest students, "I was wondering, if maybe, you had any advice to give us."

I forged a smile. Advice? From me? Why would anyone want advice from someone who doesn't have an ounce of wisdom in them? What have I done with my life? Teach? That's all. I haven't even lived, yet. I'm no different than them.

What could I possibly say to anyone that could hold any kind of meaning? I thought wildly to myself.

I tossed the words around in my head briefly and started, "Do great things."

"That's it?" chimed in another kid near the door whose leg was itching to rush out into the hallway toward the exit, but I raised my hand calmly to let him know that I wasn't finished.

"If you have even a shred of desire to succeed inside of you, I promise you, you will. But the desire to succeed is buried deep within each and every one of you. And it's up to you to find it. If you don't have the will to look for it, it'll just sit there and wilt away like a beautiful unwatered flower in the shade. Don't settle for what you already have. Fight for what you know deep in your heart, you deserve. And do great things."

And like a perfectly timed final thought to mark the end of a beloved sitcom, the bell sounded loudly and the students piled out of my room for the last time. Laila smiled at me genuinely, rushed up and gave me a hug before she left my room.

I wonder if it truly hit any of my students other than her. I wonder if my words actually meant something to the rest of them. Or if they just listened to me for the umpteen millionth time and simply allowed each part of speech I uttered to float in and out of their ears. I stood there motionless and thought about what I had just said.

The desire to succeed is buried deep within. Wilting away like a dying flower waiting to be watered. Don't settle. Fight for what you want. What you deserve.

Where in the hell did those words come from? Where do I get off telling any of my students to reach for the stars, when I myself am afraid of the dark? Why haven't I been taking my own damn advice? Why don't I take myself seriously anymore? I'm not happy with where I am or what I do. So why do I keep fucking doing it? I'm such a hypocrite. It's like I'm afraid of what's out there. It's like I'm afraid to move on to something better, for the fear of the unknown. I'm afraid of failure. Complacency has always been the captain of my life. A boat tied down to the dock will never go anywhere.

I've never gone anywhere.

One of my favorite pastimes is to look out my window after the final bell and watch all of the students rush to their buses. Especially when an unexpected rainstorm has popped up. I experience an unfathomable euphoria seeing the kids roam violently around the bus turnaround like headless chickens primed for slaughter, taking every available precaution possible to evade getting the least bit soaked. Some even have the gall to run across the grassy infield as a shortcut just to slip and fall and get drenched in muddy water. It's the funniest thing I've ever seen; the only thing capable of making me forget about the impending meeting over the status of my future.

A knock on my door took me out of the trance I was in at my window. I made my way over to it, not expecting it to be for anything or anyone important. A quick glance out the door's window to see whom it was proved futile as nobody was there. As my curiosity rose, I turned the knob and pushed it outward to examine the hallway when Darrah moved around the corner and quickly pushed me into my classroom.

"What the hell are you doing?" I blurted out in sheer surprise.

"Sit down, please."

"No thanks, I'll stand."

"You avoided me this morning."

"Yes, yes I did."

"Why?"

"Why in the fuck wouldn't I avoid you?" I asked.

"I thought we had a good time last night."

"We *did*. And that's exactly why I made every effort to avoid you. Darrah, we've been through this. I'm pretty sure that I clarified last night that I have a girlfriend and that we made a mistake."

"You did. You made it very clear. But I don't care, I want to have you right here, right now," she said as she pushed me up against the whiteboard.

"No Darrah, no. We can't do this again. I *won't* do this again. I can't."

"Are you seriously telling me that I have no effect on you right now?"

I thought about it for a moment as I looked her up and down, studying every inch of her body, as miraculous as it was my blood was no longer boiling in pent up sensual rage, "Honestly, no you don't. And I'm not even sure if you ever did."

"You have got to be joking. Your eyes drool over me every chance they get."

"Those are just my eyes, Darrah. Real men aren't complicated. We will swoon over beautiful creatures such as yourself, but what separates us from the boys is that we have enough self-control not to touch what we're looking at."

"That's real rich Jackson. That certainly wasn't the case last night after I gave you that drink I laced wi—" she said before coming to an abrupt halt, biting her tongue.

"Wait, what?"

"Nothing. I've got to get going anyway, my daughter is going to be stopping by the school with my grandson. I don't want to keep them waiting."

"No," I said as I grabbed ahold of her arm, "what did you just say?"

"Let go of me, you animal!"

"You put something in my drink last night didn't you? Didn't you bitch?" I bellowed.

"I don't have the slightest clue what you're talking about, Jackson."

"It all makes complete sense now. I can remember the rest of my night pretty easily, but that brief moment when things started to get hot and heavy are a little hazy still. You drugged me?"

"Keep telling yourself that, honey," she responded menacingly as she whipped her arm out of my grasp and stormed out the door.

I couldn't believe it. Actually, in a twisted way I could, I just didn't want to. I remember getting all fuzzy and light-headed after downing the drink she gave me. After that everything was a blur, until I came to and ran out of the club in a frenzy for having allowed the unforgivable to happen. Beautiful women are the most hideous of monsters. Their whole egregious existence is solely meant to destroy any and all men who cross their path. They'll chew you up until you're nothing but mush in their mouth and spit out all of your bones, all 206 of them. But they'll keep the one that fills out the bulge in our pants to pick the remaining flesh out of their teeth.

T wo o'clock had come and gone. I wasn't even sure if I wanted to attend this pointless meeting with Führer Raker and the Administrative team. It wasn't likely to contain any good news for me. I'm sure that she has stopped at nothing to ensure I'm put in my place. Why should I attend something that will just piss me off more than I already am lately? My life already feels like it's gone to hell in a hand basket in less than 48 hours. I can only imagine this meeting would be the icing on the metaphorical cake.

After having heard my name called over the intercom every couple of minutes, for nearly ten minutes, I realized I wasn't going to be able to hide from the inevitable. They would find me and castrate me, whether I showed up or not. Might as well get whatever horrifying news they've got to tell me straight from the Devil's mouth rather than hearing it through the walls of the school. The walls of every school can talk. And they never shut the fuck up. Always be wary of what you say in a school. The walls listen in on every conversation. They take detailed notes. They're capable of cruel judgment. And then they pass the information along to the first person willing to stop and listen to what it has to say. It travels around the building with the ease of the basilisk from the second Harry Potter novel spewing its judgment of every living creature held within its clutches.

There's no escaping the clutches of the school walls, especially the walls of the Principal's Conference Room.

The receptionist in Student Affairs, Ms. Tenley escorted me to the Conference Room for my "appointment" which I was casually twelve minutes late for.

Of course Mrs. Raker would be the one to take the lead in my impending execution. She'd already set up the gallows and was primed to place my head inside the noose, "Ah Mr. Cain, how thoughtful of you to finally join us. You must be without a clock in your classroom."

"Well, I have requested a new one numerous times after all, since it's still an hour behind," I declared sarcastically, but truthfully.

"Right then, let's get this started since you're errant lack of courtesy for everyone in this room has put us behind schedule. Please, take a seat."

"Thanks, I'd rather stand."

Principal Powell, who was probably the only individual in this increasingly shrinking room that I actually liked, and with whom I respected greatly walked gracefully toward my position near the door. He put his arm around my shoulder and whispered gently, "Please, Jack."

I caved in immediately and allowed Principal Powell to escort me to the seat nearest him. I could feel the room continuing to grow smaller, while six sets of eyes pierced me with burning daggers.

They were all my executioners. Every last one of them were dressed in their Sunday's finest, ready to pull their black hoods over their faces and seal my fate. Everyone except for Principal Powell who was dressed like a priest in his clerical collar reciting scriptures and tossing Hail Mary's into the pit of my misfortune in a last ditch effort to save my wretched soul from almost certain damnation.

"Mr. Cain," proclaimed Mrs. Raker, "Do you know why we called this urgent meeting today?"

I looked around the room uneasily at the many faces who appeared highly uninterested in anything I would have to say.

"Yes. A little birdy told me it was regarding my future," I said as I stared directly at Mrs. Ellis, who promptly looked down at the papers scattered in front of her as she pretended to read something.

"That's right. And how do you feel you have been doing during your tenure here as a teacher Mr. Cain?"

I thought about it for a moment, but before I could utter a word, Mrs. Raker answered her own question.

"On second thought, don't waste your breath Mr. Cain, as this isn't a trial, it's more of a sentencing. I will tell you exactly how you've been doing during the duration of your tenure. With the exception of your first two years, which could pass for adequate to acceptable, this past year has been nothing short of a disgrace. You give teachers a bad name, Mr. Cain. You don't appear to care about your job, you never attend any professional development trainings or after school meetings unless prompted to do so, you hardly interact with any other teachers or the parents of your students, and quite frankly your professionalism both inside the classroom in your interactions with your students and outside the classroom with your colleagues and superiors is absolutely atrocious. In light of recent events, we have officially come to the decision to revoke our initial offer of allowing you back as a teacher here at North Grayson High School next year. Your performance has suffered mightily over the past year and your attitude has simply been dreadful."

I was at a complete loss for words. I knew bad news was coming, but I didn't know it would be taken this far. I half expected to be put on probation and be forced to take additional trainings and be observed ten additional times a year, and maybe even take a pay cut. But to basically be relieved of my teaching duties? That was a shock. That was a slap in the face. With all of the shitty human beings at this school, I was the only one being let go? And it was all because one bitch didn't like me. What a fucked up world American education is.

They opened the hatchback doors of the gallows and let me plunge to my death. I thought maybe they'd watch me squirm and periodically gasp for every morsel of air before cutting the rope and offering me a second chance, an alternative. But these executioners were only willing to watch me die. Not suffer.

"I don't even get a say in the matter? Mr. Powell," I looked at my only source of hope in the room, my eyes pleading with him to speak up on my behalf, "isn't there another way? Don't I get to plead my case at all? I mean, this is my life we're talking about here. My only source of income."

"It's completely out of my hands, Jack. Their vote was regrettably unanimous," Mr. Powell said sullenly.

"With all due respect Mr. Cain," Mrs. Raker spoke up as she started to put my files away her in folder and get out of her seat, "this congregation doesn't care to hear your explanations or pleas for your job. The decision is final and this meeting is over."

"With all due respect Mrs. Raker," I interjected lowly, "my apologies, *Jasmine*, you can go fuck yourself."

Mrs. Raker fumed with anger, and I could almost see the smoke emitting from every orifice of her face. I stormed out of the Conference Room feverishly listening to the lingering gasps from the other executioners who sat stoic in disbelief, as they choked trying to digest my words. I furiously made my way through the office hallways and crashed through the front door into the parking lot.

"Jackson, is that you?" came a sweet angelic voice from behind me.

I couldn't quite put my finger on it, but that voice sounded unbelievably familiar. Despite the rage pulsating throughout my body I slowly turned around toward the main lobby doors as a beautiful woman with flowing brown hair was walking out with a small child.

As she got closer my heart began to race in excitement and terror as my eyes were finally able to make out who she was.

"Darlene? What in the world are you doing here?" I asked.

She flashed a smile, "I feel like I should be asking you the same question. I heard them page a

Jackson in there and I couldn't help but wonder if it was you or someone else. This is completely bizarre."

I forced a smile, "I'm here because I work here. Well, I did anyway. I'm likely going to be working elsewhere next year."

The small child Darlene was carrying reached out his left hand and touched my arm. I looked down at him and Darlene gracefully pulled his hand away.

"Sorry about that."

"No, no it's perfectly okay. And who is this little guy?" I asked as I started to make funny faces at the little boy, which made him smile and laugh.

"This is my son, Carter, Jr."

"Carter?"

"Yes, I named him…after his father."

"Oh, that's nice. How old is he?"

"He's three."

"And," I started but instantly stopped myself to make sure I picked the appropriate words, "is the father in the picture?"

She smiled nervously, "Oh no, he's never met his father. I don't think his father even knows he was born. You see," she put little Carter down on his feet and lightly held her hands over his ears, "he was the result of a little one night fling I had."

I nodded in understanding as Darlene started toward the parking lot, but I followed her, "Wait, you never told me what you're doing here? I mean, you're a long ways from Framingham."

She chuckled, "I don't live there anymore, silly. I live in South Carolina now. I'm just down here for the week. I decided to stop in here to visit my mother. She works here you know."

We stopped in front of her car, "She does? Who is your mother, if you don't mind my asking?"

She buckled little Carter into his car seat and shut the door before coming back around to me, "Darrah Meadows. She's worked here for a few years, and I've always meant to come down and visit her but I've just never had the time."

Her words hit me like a sniper's bullet. I didn't know how to react to what she'd just said. I wasn't even sure if I'd heard it correctly.

"Darrah Meadows is your mother? Your last name is Meadows?" I asked trying to conceal my astonishment.

"Yeah, why?"

"No reason. I do know her. She's a lovely woman."

"You don't need to lie, I know how she can be. On face value she acts like a saint, but underneath she can turn bat shit crazy in no time. That's why I lived with my grandparents up in Framingham while she was down here."

"Well, it was really nice to see you, for whatever that's worth. Seeing your face actually has lifted my spirits a little bit today."

"I'm glad I could do that. Is there any reason why we couldn't maybe go out to dinner or something later? To catch up?" she asked as she bit her lip.

Worry crept across my face. I could tell where such a night would end up going. Her mother had pulled the same line with me the other day.

"I really wish I could, but I'm not sure if my girlfriend would approve."

She lowered her head, "I can understand that. Well, I'll be in town for a few more days. I'm staying at the Pinewood Suites. Perhaps we'll run into each other again."

"I sincerely hope so," I said.

She gently touched my shoulder as she got into the driver's side of her car. I watched her talk with her son briefly before starting up the vehicle and inching forward. She still looked magnificent even after all this time. She rolled down her window and her son's window in the back as I waved and started to turn around.

"Say goodbye to your da—I mean, Mr. Cain, Carter," Darlene said and the kid instantly waved and smiled.

Before I could even react to what she'd started to say she was gone and out of the gated perimeter. I stood in complete silence as her car disappeared into the distance.

Was she going to say what I think she was going to say? I hope she was simply fooling with me or caught herself from saying something she wanted to be true that wasn't. After all she said she's named her son after his father. Last I checked my name wasn't Carter nor has it ever been.

Oh shit, but it *was* in college. She found me at that party and called me Carter because that was the pseudonym I used for my poetry. She thought that was my name for the longest time.

And all of sudden, I was back in a shitty mood. No job, no future, and a bastard love child. Nothing a few hundred drinks couldn't make me forget.

Instead of going directly home after my dramatic exit from school, I immediately went to Ray's Pub and successfully connived Perry into joining me. The only thing I wanted to do was drink, and forget that my problems even existed. Forget that *I* existed. I wanted to pump so much alcohol into my body that my blood would magically transform into every lager I've ever poured into my system. I wanted to piss alcohol.

"You look like shit, my man," Perry greeted me at the bar, "what the hell is wrong with you?"

"Believe it or not, that's the second time I've been told that…*this* week. You're looking at the newest ousted teacher at NGHS," I replied.

"Get the fuck outta here, they torched your ass?"

"No, I'm technically still employed at the moment. I get to finish out the year tomorrow, but next year yes, I'm completely out of a job."

"That fucking sucks, dude. I don't wanna be stuck there with all those shitty people. You're the only one I can almost deal with," he divulged, "and even you suck on your best days."

That comment managed to get a chuckle out of me, but only a small one as I focused more on downing my fifth beer in only twenty minutes.

"Also, I apparently have a child. A three year old."

"Quit busting my balls."

"I'm serious," I choked on the words, "a former love interest of mine from college happened to show up at the school today with her kid, and she kind of let it slip that he might be mine."

"Are you fucking serious?"

"Dead ass."

"That's crazy my man. I don't know what I'd do if that shit happened to me."

"That's why I'm here drowning in my sorrows, one beer at a time," I said as finished another beer in only seconds.

"You better slow down, Jack," Perry urged, "you'll end up making a trip to the emergency room if you keep downing 'em like that."

"Don't worry about it, I already told the bartender to cut me off when it looks like I have no depth perception."

"Fair enough. So you got anything else you wanna tell me?" Perry asked.

"Not that I know of," I stared at him quizzically as my vision started to create two fuzzy likenesses of him.

He pulled out a picture and slid it over to me, "Explain that."

"Where the fuck did you get that?" I demanded as I stared nervously at the picture he had just handed me. A picture of Darrah and I at Peeper's the other night.

"Everybody's got 'em! They were in everybody's mailboxes after school. What the fuck did you do?"

Things were just getting worse, "Darrah invited me to dinner the other night, as friends, so I went. Turns out she actually asked me to watch her strip at Peeper's," I sighed loudly as I passed the photo back to Perry.

"Dude, that's fan-fucking-tastic! Damn. Did you do her?"

"No, I didn't *do* her! I have a girlfriend you jackass."

"Oh," he sounded disappointed, like my cock was his cock and I had just denied him sexual gratification, "because she was telling everybody that you two fucked in a backroom and that she told you it wasn't a good idea because you had a girlfriend. But you insisted, so she caved."

"Are you fucking serious?"

"Yeah, man. I'm not gonna lie, I saw a lot of pissed off female faces in that mailroom when she was telling them the story. I don't know if I'd go back to that school tomorrow, if I were you. They'll be like a pack of rabid vaginas ready to tear you to shreds for cheating. I can't believe you did that."

"I *didn't* do it! She's making shit up," I yelled and then downed another glass of beer, "I went there for dinner, we talked and that was it."

Perry was reading my face intently trying to determine if I was telling the truth or if the booze was trying to mask my denial. I hoped my facial muscles would remain stoic enough to not give me away.

"If you say so, prick. But if you did do anything, I commend you man, because she is one hot piece of ass. Even if she is bat shit crazy."

"This is just perfect. Could this week get any worse?"

Perry choked on his drink, "Don't tempt fate there, buddy. Even if you're being rhetorical, fate will politely take it as a challenge and fuck shit up even more for you. Just sit there, wallow in your sorrows, and have another beer. Or five."

"That's what I plan to do."

"Oh no, better idea," Perry interjected as the bartender looked at me as if I were getting extremely close to my limit, "why don't you come with me to SAA?"

"What?" I asked bewildered.

"Sex Addicts Anonymous. It was your idea that you planted in my mind yesterday. I looked into it. Enough with these high school girls, I'm moving on to the real prizes. The ones who wanna fuck because it's a disease they're trying to cope with."

"You do realize most of these people actually go to these meetings seeking help, right? They're not all there because they're looking to feed their addiction."

"That's what you think. I know for a fact, it's probably a front for everybody. They're all looking to score. I wouldn't be surprised if I bag me a couple of horny chicks tonight," Perry announced assuredly.

"Whatever you say, dick. I don't want any part of it. If I went to that, I would just dig myself into a deeper hole if my girlfriend ever found out. I'm not even sure how she's going to react to the news about me possibly being a father."

"Well that's an easy one, you don't tell her. But anyway, it's your loss if you don't go, fag. More pussy for me then," Perry joked as he got up from his seat and tossed a Benjamin at the bartender, "Hey chief, here's my tab. Use the extra to get my friend here a cab when you cut him off."

The bartender nodded and took the money, setting some aside after ringing in Perry's tab. Perry patted me on the back and gave me a softhearted "I feel your pain" look and darted out of the bar into the sun setting evening.

"Another round," I probed the bartender who was viciously cleaning out a mug with a towel. He looked at me with a grimace and reluctantly poured me another drink before returning to his line of mugs.

"Something got you down?" came an eerily familiar voice from a few stools down at the bar.

I shakily glanced in the direction of the voice and a bright blue suede vest blinded my drunken eyes.

"Carter Corrish? What in blue blazes brings you around these parts?"

"Nothing specifically. I just happened to be in the area and decided to stop by for a quick drink before heading back out on the road. You look terrible my friend. What's wrong with you?" he asked sounding surprisingly concerned.

"Do you recall our little conversation the other night?" I slurred.

"I do, rather vividly. It was the only intriguing conversation I had that day."

"I take back what I said."

He looked at me with overwhelming shock, "I beg your pardon?"

"You were right, I was wrong. There's no God. There just can't be after all that's been happening to me."

"As much as I would love to congratulate you on switching to a more rational view on life and morality, I simply cannot do so. You're drunk, Jackson. You wouldn't be saying that, if you weren't."

"Look Carter, I may sound drunk and appear drunk," I burped in between my words, "but I'm thinking clearly. As clear as the horizon after a summer's rain."

"If you say so," he muttered as he shook his head feverishly.

"I'm having trouble letting go."

"Of what?"

"Everything. Even though I've hated every aspect of my life over the past year, it's all I knew. I mean, what am I going to do now? I don't have a clue. What's going to happen to me? I don't know that either. This would all be so much easier to deal with, if it were *me* making the decisions, y'know? I'm so fucking tired of having everyone else decide my path for me. It's been that way since I was a little kid, and I'm absolutely sick of it," I declared valiantly.

"I can understand that. Too many people feel the need to control everything. While the rest of us are just pawns to their evil deeds. It's no way to live, that's for damn sure."

"I just don't care anymore."

"And why's that?"

"Because it doesn't matter. None of this does. It shouldn't matter. I've got nothing holding me down anymore. I'm a lonely leaf floating in the wind. No longer am I attached to the tree that's rooted to the ground. I'm free to go wherever. I don't care *anymore*. And even better than that, I don't care that I don't care."

"That's deep, Jackson. So what happened, if you don't mind my asking, that's got you so down and drastically changing your perspective on things?" he asked with a quiet smile and a hint of intrigue in his voice.

I hesitated and breathed heavily, "I don't really want to get into it, Carter. It'll just drain even more out of me. I'd rather just forget it and move on. But let's just say, that the very foundation of my life is crumbling beneath me."

"Well, if I may be so bold," he said as he leaned in a little bit closer to me, "maybe it's crumbling, so that you can build something better in its place."

And with that remark Carter got up from his stool, placed his hand on my arm and squeezed it tightly. He laid his journal down on the stool beside me and headed out the door. That was the last time I ever saw him. I looked down at the journal and then up at the bartender. He was eyeing me even more intently than he was earlier.

"You okay fella?"

"A little tipsy. But yeah, I'd have to say I'm still holding strong. Why?"

"Who the hell were you talking to?" he asked affrightedly.

"Oh, just now? That was my friend Carter."

"Who?"

"Carter Corrish," I responded irritably, "that guy that just left."

"I don't know what you're talking about, man, but you were just talking to yourself for the past couple of minutes."

"What are you nuts? I was talking to that guy just now."

"That's exactly what I was thinking," he started as he stared a hole right through me, "I don't know what you think just happened, but nobody's been in here since your friend that gave me the hundred left."

I was suffering an extreme case of bewilderment. My head was pounding and in excruciating pain. I had no idea what this guy was talking about. How could he not see Carter? I mean, he was *just* here. He even left his journal.

I opened the front cover of Carter's journal and the inscription freaked me out a little bit. I was unsure if I was seeing things because I was drunk, or if I was actually seeing what was written on the page. *Property of Jackson Cain.* Just underneath my name I saw the initials C.C.

That can't be there. This was *his* journal not mine.

I flipped through the pages and saw nothing scribbled on any of the pages except the first page. A simple message was scrawled across the top margin: *Remember your past, remember your dreams. Keep moving toward the horizon and write your future, it's in your hands. It's always been in your hands.* I had no idea what to make of it. Nothing made sense anymore. My head continued to throb in unbearable pain, as that wound up being the last thing I could remember from that night.

After Carter's David Copperfield vanishing act, and the bartender calling me crazy, I blacked out in a drunken stupor on the counter. I'm not 100% sure how I got home. The only thing I was certain of was that I would likely be alone, since Janice had her Book Club meeting. I'm normally alone anyway, whether she's physically there or not. She wouldn't be interested in seeing me like this. If she were home I would have no choice but to sleep on the couch. That's *if* she were home.

I pulled up to the school approximately 30 minutes after it had begun and parked near the front of the building. There's no doubt that they found a sub for me when they noticed I hadn't arrived. Like I would show up at a reasonable time after having had my future terminated the day before.

I pushed open the door to my '77 Camaro, and walked back to pop open the trunk. What a glorious sight to behold. A Daewoo Precision Industries USAS-12 with ten detachable 20-drum magazines capable of firing 400 rounds per minute, and an M16A4 Assault rifle with ten Beta C-Mag 100-round double-lobed drums capable of firing 750 rounds per minute.

The Grinch and the Joker have got nothing on my smile on this day.

I stocked up on all the ammunition I could manage to hold in my backpack while I placed the M16A4 over my shoulder. I walked maniacally toward the front entrance while I clicked the first magazine into the USAS-12.

It was surprisingly quiet for the last day of school. There weren't any kids arriving late and standing at the front doors, nor were there any kids inside the office waiting to be admitted into the building. Made it all the more easier for me to sneak in relatively unnoticed at first. I scanned my key fob at the main office doors and the door unlocked. The receptionist and the attendance monitor who were normally sitting at the main desk were nowhere in sight.

This was my only chance. It's as if God was giving me my lone opportunity to enter the school unnoticed. Operation Fuck Everything Up was right on schedule.

I scurried through the side entrance into the main lobby adjacent to the auditorium and saw a few students at the end of the hall making their way around the panther statue and out of sight. Maybe I should head up the stairwell and start in the upstairs classrooms and make my way down. Or maybe I should pull the fire alarm and pick off everyone as they rush out of the building to safety. Or maybe I should just walk back out to my car and careen it off a cliff like Thelma & Louise, sparing the lives of everyone in this shit hole.

But I spent a lot on this ammunition. So somebody has to pay. Why am I the only one who has to suffer? I will not be held prisoner by my misfortunes. It's go time.

I busted through the stairwell doors and made my ascent up the concrete slabs. I'm not sure why, but at that moment I was overcome with a joy I'd never felt before. I started to whistle a little Bobby McFerrin and the tune echoed gleefully throughout the stairwell. Before I made it to the top steps the door opened. A freshman, small in stature and red in the face, stopped dead in his tracks and dropped his books in a panic to the floor: my first victim.

My finger lightly grazed the trigger of my USAS-12 and out poured an onslaught of shells bent on utter destruction. The young kid's body lurched backward and slammed into the wall knocking plaster to the floor, as entry wound after entry wound magically appeared on the front of his torso.

Overcome with blissful emotion I started to sing, "In every life we have some trouble, when you worry you make it double," I crooned.

I slowly walked by his lifeless body and saw him desperately wheezing for air, "Don't worry, be happy," I chirped before blasting open the doors to the second floor with an array of scattered bullets.

"No more worries, pal," I mumbled to the bleeding corpse as I delicately placed the barrel against his temple and pulled once more on the trigger watching his soul vanish from his eyes, "You're welcome."

The sound of my USAS-12 was deafening and echoed loudly throughout the stairwell which prompted the teachers from the nearby classrooms to come rushing out in to the hallway. Teachers, they never miss a beat. My next victims were right on cue.

As soon as they entered the hallway, I greeted them with an assortment of bullets straight to every fraction of their bodies from their legs to their chests to their heads, as I moved like a playground swing going back and forth after being caught in a hurricane. Students stupidly poured out of their respective rooms to check on the commotion and were caught in the crossfire. Body after body fell motionless to the floor as round after round penetrated this student and that student and this teacher and that teacher.

"Cause when you worry your face will frown, and that will bring everybody down," I belted out as I changed magazines.

I pulled the fire alarm and watched even more classrooms full of students and staff pour into the hallway where they were promptly greeted by Tony Montana reincarnated.

"So don't worry, be happy!"

I felt like I was living a Quentin Tarantino movie. It was so surreal. *I* was the executioner now. *I* was the decider of everyone's fate. No longer was I caught in the crosshairs of other people's power. I made the rules now.

The upstairs hallways were transformed into a battleground as people fled the sound of my USAS-12. The screams of terror were so hauntingly loud they shivered me to my core like nails on a chalkboard as more and more skeletons tumbled to their mutilated demise. Bodies upon bodies covered the graveyard of the halls as I continued my meticulous march through every nook and cranny of North Grayson High.

I popped in the last magazine for the USAS-12 and peppered the walls and classroom doors with bullets hoping there would be judgmental pricks barricaded on the other side officially meeting their maker. I sprayed the walls with destruction like a Jackson Pollock painting until I heard an empty *click! click! click!* which caused me to discard my trusty shotgun.

I walked into room 1202, which was completely empty. Desks were overturned and thousands of papers were scattered across the linoleum floor as I uncontrollably disrobed my backpack and emptied it of its ammunition. I prepped my M16A4 Assault rifle before poking my head out of the window, which had a perfect view of the parking lot. The entire perimeter of the building was flooded with people, students and staff rushing to safety and police officers and SWAT team personnel pulling up frantically toward the front entrance. The streets were completely sealed off. Nobody allowed in and nobody allowed out.

I slowly eased the window open, so as not to draw much attention to myself from down below. I hardly took much notice, but caught a glimpse of a robin as it landed on the edge of windowsill, moved its head in all different directions in a matter of seconds, and then flew away. I was unaware if anyone outdoors knew specifically where I was located in the building, so I wanted to exercise as much precaution as possible. This can't end. Not yet. I propped my body up on top of the counter space directly below the window and placed each magazine out in a row on the windowsill for easy access. Very conscientiously I poked the head of the assault rifle out the base of the window and pulled the trigger.

It was a fireworks attraction.

No one ducked for cover right away, at least not until they were hit. No one knew where they were coming from, but everyone was intrigued to find out. When the crowd of people realized what was happening, they sought shelter but couldn't find any. The bullets were spitting out the barrel of my M16A4 at suicidal speed, leaving death and destruction on the cusp of everything it struck.

Vehicles were given new décor, sirens were permanently silenced, and screams and cries for help were all drowned out by the sound of each bullet making contact with its intended target. Bodies lay in pools of crimson on the concrete. The parking lot would forever be a reminder of death and decay, much like the hallways of the second floor. The entire grounds of the school would inevitably become a memorial. They would need to tear it down and relocate or else constantly be reminded of the events of this day. A day that would live in infamy.

Dead student here. Dying teacher there. Wounded officer here. Sinful souls forever cleansed of all their transgressions and suffering.

No one was safe as I popped in magazine after magazine and unleashed the fury of Hell. *Terminated you say?* Consider this my resignation. Consider this my parting gift to you all.

The door behind me burst open as I finished the last magazine of my M16A4. I turned around sharply and saw the SWAT team enter the classroom at full force. But they weren't going to take me without a fight. I reached into my army vest pocket as if I had a pistol and yanked my empty hand out to greet the SWAT team. Each member opened fire at my bulletproof vest-less body as blood squirted out of each wound their automatic weapons inflicted. I fell to the floor from the countertop with the nerves in my right hand forcing it to stay glued in the form of a handgun.

Blood gushed out of my mouth and I could feel my breathing getting more and more labored as my lungs gasped for air. The bloody bullet holes in my chest instantly stained the grey alma mater shirt from my senior year of high school I was wearing under my vest. I'm not sure how many people I killed, but it had to have been a lot. There is no mercy given to those who don't deserve it.

"Why'd you do it, chief?" asked one of the SWAT officers as he approached me slowly, still with his weapon drawn, "Why did you do this? Huh? Why?"

"Why not?" I gasped as I coughed up more blood.

"Because it's inhumane. I hope you enjoy an eternity in Hell."

"I was already…in Hell," I started, as the air was slowly disappearing from my lungs, "At least…I'll be going somewhere…I'm familiar with. Thank…you."

The SWAT officer bowed his head in disgust and mercifully fired one last round at my forehead as it slammed into the concrete at the force of the bullet.

It was finally over.

The alarm clock angrily sounded and my body lurched into consciousness as my head pounded with an immense migraine. I was in my bed, alone. Still. Janice's side of the bed remained untouched and unruffled. I guess she didn't come home last night. Wouldn't have been the first time. Seems like at least twice a month she stays the night at a friend's or her mother's house without the common decency of letting me know.

I strolled out of the bedroom with the particular gait of a one-legged zombie. My head was pounding unlike anything I'd ever experienced. Must've been an intense dream. Too bad I can't remember any of it.

The apartment was still dark as I made my way to the fridge in the kitchen. A beer would be the ideal drink to start my day. I can still feel the effects from last night. Might as well stay drunk. My last official day as an employed teacher. A blood alcohol content of .16 might actually get me through it.

I grabbed the orange juice instead and closed the door of the fridge when the kitchen light abruptly turned on startling me. I was blinded by it but I could vaguely make out the silhouette standing near the switch. It was Janice. Arms crossed and an intense look of displeasure etched across her face.

"Hey there, stranger!" I sleepily said as I leaned in for a kiss, which prompted Janice to turn her head away.

"Save it, Jack."

I glanced toward the door and noticed a few boxes with a bunch of my things tossed into them. A couple of empty bins and boxes were perched against the wall. I felt like I was still dreaming, as the confusion caused my head to pound even more.

"What's with all the boxes? And why are my things in them?" I asked.

"I said save it, Jack. Where did you go Monday night?"

"I went out to dinner," I said, which was partially true, "because you were out doing whatever it was you were doing."

"Don't you dare make this about me, when it's my issue with you! Who is *this*?"

She put a picture down on the table in front of me. I rubbed my eyes and picked it up. It was the picture of Darrah and me…at Peepers. Oh, shit. But where did she get it? How did it end up in her hands? Did Darrah print enough copies to the Postal Service to send out for the whole damn world to see?

"Um, it's a work colleague of mine," I said, which again was partially true. She wasn't a colleague *then*, but earlier in the day she was.

"Don't you dare fucking lie to me, you bastard!" Janice interrupted, "You expect me to believe that trash? She looks like a stripper to me, Jack."

"That's her second job. She really is a colleague," I said firmly, adding fuel to the fire without even realizing it.

"Shut up. Just shut the fuck up! Did you do anything with this slut? And do not lie to me. Don't destroy the shred of dignity I still have for you."

"No, I didn't," I mumbled.

"Wrong answer, Jack. I know you did. This bitch told me. I'm done. I'm done with us. Get the fuck out of my sight. Don't bother coming home after you're out of work. I'll have all of your stuff out on the curb, you can pick it up out there."

Just when you think you've hit rock bottom, life laughs maniacally, tosses you a shovel and tells you to keep digging.

I wanted to say something to try to mend the broken pieces of what might have been left of our relationship. I wanted to tell her that I left the club in a frenzy and stopped what likely would have been more, all because I had thought of her. But I knew despite anything I said, she wouldn't have it. So I said nothing. A man knows when to stop. He knows when a woman is at her wits end. A smart man anyway. A stupid man would just keep piling it on until the woman grows three hundred feet tall and starts demolishing half the city.

I wasted no time in getting ready for my last day. I skipped a shower and rapidly put my clothes on, wrapping my tie around my neck as I grabbed my bag and headed for the door. I wanted out of that apartment as quickly as possible. No need to put down another layer of bricks on a crumbling foundation. It's time to just let it cave in on itself and buy a new plot of land.

As I reached for the door handle, Janice put a hand on my shoulder and stopped me, "Wait, just a second."

"What?" I asked with a mixed tone of hope and denial.

"I haven't been completely honest with you either."

"You haven't?" I responded with little conviction.

"No. I've been cheating on you ever since we started dating. A few co-workers, some people I've met, and just the other night, this God of a man, Gibbs. I have an addiction, Jack. Those Book Club meetings I go to every week, they don't exist."

I knew exactly where this was going, "You're telling me you're a sex addict? That's your justification for cheating on me all this time? Are you fucking nuts?"

"Shut the fuck up! You cheated too, you sneaky bastard! I have an addiction, you piece of shit! You don't! That means you cheated knowingly and were a willing participant! Your transgression is far worse than mine! So don't even think about trying to make me sound worse than you, because I'm not!"

"In what sick twisted fantasy mindfuck of a universe does that logic even make any sense, Janice? Are you fucking listening to yourself?"

"Get the fuck out of here! I never want to see you again!" she shouted as she slapped me across the face and pushed me out of the apartment.

I was immensely invigorated as the muscles in my forearms began to contract and expand in a furious rage. My fists curled up into little balls and I wanted punch something, anything. The wall, the door, Janice. Everyone she's fucked.

Older generations, like those of our grandparents could solve any issue that life threw at them. Probably even my current predicament. They had life figured out. They stayed together through tough times because that's what you were supposed to do. You wouldn't throw away a brand new shirt simply because you got a stain on it. You would put it in the wash and attempt to get the stain out. You shouldn't quit on someone just because life decides to throw you a few curveballs.

Perhaps what made it easier for our grandparents was the fact that they didn't have thousands of people "following" them, addictively remarking on their every move, and constantly liking their pictures and status updates whenever their relationships got difficult.

Today when our relationships hit rock bottom, instead of talking it out and getting to the route of the issues, we just login to the social media websites that consume our lives and get high off of a false sense of security and appreciation. We value our worth based on the comments of strangers and inboxed messages filled with hollow words that have no depth or immediate value. Meanwhile, the person you should be focusing on, the one who sees you when there is no filter on your face becomes an option, while the rest of the world who only sees your photoshopped exterior becomes the priority.

Our grandparents didn't lose what was real by chasing what only appeared to be. They actually worked at fixing what was broken, a trait that has all but disappeared over the evolution of time.

I know I shouldn't quit. Maybe she deserves another chance. Maybe we both do. Deep down, I know I should do everything I can to fill the fractured pieces of our relationship with love's adhesive. But I just can't. I don't have it inside of me. I'm inches away from throwing in the towel.

I mean she had been cheating on me ever since we started dating. That's over a year of infidelity. That's over a year of sneaking around and lying. How can anyone be okay with that? She kicked me out of the apartment for good and threw all of my shit in boxes. I can't even believe what's happened. *She* cheats hundreds, maybe thousands of times from an apparent "addiction." I cheat once and *I* get kicked to the curb.

Sex is an addiction. I'll give her that one. It is. Anyone who has had sex can't tell you that it's not addicting. It feels really, really good. Good things are just as addictive as bad things. Sex is probably the closest that human beings get to experiencing some form of Heaven on Earth. But I don't care what she or anyone says, an addiction to sex doesn't give anyone the right to cheat and not feel any kind of regret.

Cheating is cheating, end of story.

I sat in my Camaro at the red light on the Loman Parkway intersection for what felt like an eternity. My mind was nothing more than a beautiful stained glass window with every brittle piece of color representing a small chunk of my life that was ready to break. Emotions flooded through my pores, drowning every morsel of logical judgment.

I wanted to die.

My career was over, my relationship was ending, and my future was bleak. One can only carry around so much bullshit on their shoulders before they finally collapse from the weight of it.

The timeline of my life started to replay in my mind as tears started to roll down my cheeks. I remembered my younger days in Belmont, my college days at Guildford, and my early years in Florida. They were all filled with so much life and so much promise. How could all of that lead me to this moment here? Why was God getting so much satisfaction in my suffering? If one thing goes wrong, everything does.

All I wanted to do was drive my car as fast as I possibly could and careen it off a bridge and just end it. Colton did. His father did. I could too.

I revved the engine and looked around. I was going to do it. I was going to drive my car into oncoming traffic. But it was eerily quiet on the roads, unlike most mornings. The roads were empty, and the light remained red. I glanced over at the bus stop bench to look at the homeless man for one final time but noticed he wasn't there.

There was a knock on my passenger's side window that startled me back into reality. I wiped a few tears from off my face and looked out the window. It was the homeless man. I rolled the glass down.

"Excuse me sir, I couldn't help but notice that you've missed at least three green lights already. I wanted to make sure everything was okay?" the homeless man asked.

I sniffed loudly and spoke up in a broken tone, "I'm...I'm okay. Thank you."

"You sure? You don't look okay."

"I'm fine. I promise."

"No, I don't think you are. I've seen that look on a man's face before."

"What look?" I asked bewildered.

"That look," he leaned in through the window and tilted the rearview down toward my face, "I've seen it a hundred times. That's the look one has when they feel like they've got nothing worth living for."

I looked hard in the mirror and saw exactly what he was talking about. My eyes were barren shells of what they used to be. They were filled with nothing but despair and emptiness. My face was hardly recognizable. I didn't even look like the same man I used to be. I was someone else entirely.

"I know it probably don't mean much coming from me, but between the two of us, I could have ended it a thousand times over the last year and a half that I've been out here. But I never did."

"Why didn't you?"

"Because this is the only chance at life we get sir. Yeah, things might be bad now, but that don't mean they always will be. There's always tomorrow. And the possibility of a better tomorrow being just hours away, gets me through the hardest moments. All you need is just one daisy to grow in a field full of weeds, my man. Just one daisy can turn it all around."

I didn't know what it was about what this man said that hit a trigger with me, but his words had an impact. The sadness in my expression started to slowly dissipate. The man flashed a quick smile and lightly tapped on the edge of my window and turned around toward the bus stop as the light turned green.

I waved at him and returned the smile as I drove off. I thought of everything that had gone wrong recently at school and pushed it deep down into my stomach. I thought of Colton and his dad and wished that I could've been there in the moments they took their lives so that I could try to stop them, to make them see that it could get better down the road.

You just have to get in your car and drive a little ways to find out.

The last day of school and my NGHS teaching career had arrived.

A storm was brewing in the sky *and* the pit of my stomach. Clouds as black as the rivers that run straight to Hell consumed the inlay of the horizon where North Grayson High sat perched amongst a valley of nothingness. It was about to go down. Oh, how it was about to go down in dramatic fashion.

I don't typically bring my home life with me to school. I don't like to burden anybody with my personal problems. It's unprofessional. Just unnecessary added stress, and quite frankly, the kids don't care either. They feign interest in our social lives much in the same way we do theirs.

How was your weekend class?

A particularly hollow question that I leave open-ended for anyone to answer, which is always followed by a multitude of incomprehensible blabber that I'm not even remotely interested in hearing to begin with. I just nod and smile, giving the illusion that I actually give a shit, when I don't.

I don't expect my students to care what's wrong with me. And I don't care if they care. But by God, do I hope they enjoy the show because today, everything has caught up to me.

I've been strategically evading dealing with my personal problems all year, all my life actually, but like a bloodthirsty serial killer in a B-rate slasher film it has finally caught up to me. The endless dark that has threatened to engulf me my whole life has devoured me like in my adolescent dreams. My problems just continued to pile up over time and there's no more room in the garbage heap of my life. I've tripped over my own lies and mishaps trying to get away just to find myself in the clutches of the undeniable truth. My life is Hell. As long as I'm still here, it's nothing but Hell.

Everything has gone wrong this week. More wrong than normal, that is. People I thought I could trust have shown me their true colors. That goes for me too.

I feel like an uncharacteristically nervous contestant at a talent show who has completely forgotten his entire routine, standing there bug-eyed with a warped expression of embarrassment hoping he'll wake up from his nightmare. The only problem is, my nightmare won't go away no matter how often I push it aside. My nightmare isn't simply the chemical reactions in my brain creating an alternate reality where everything is completely fucked up. I haven't stumbled down the rabbit hole this is *real* life. No matter how tightly I squeeze my eyelids shut, I know that when I open them the same miserable existence I have been living will still be staring back at me through the shattered mirror of my hopes and dreams, laughing uncontrollably at the disgust strewn across my face.

The parking lot was eerily quiet, as was the norm when you arrive at the last possible second. All of the parking spots were filled which forced me to take whatever was left. There was little to no commotion in the morning mist outside of the building. The hustle and bustle and inner workings of Hell were inside those walls.

I strolled unenthusiastically across the lot toward the front entrance when out of the corner of my eye a beat up station wagon caught my attention. The passenger side door opened up and a skinny black girl with a slightly masked black eye stepped out in a pseudo-presentable white dress. I couldn't believe who it was as she smiled at me.

"Daneesha? Is that you?" I asked the girl as I crept closer to the building.

"Yes it is, Mr. Cain," she replied as she tried to smooth out the ruffles in her dress, "I thought about what you's said tha other night. I's got an appointment to talk with a counselor about lettin' me come back next year to finish ma senior year."

On a day where everything inside of me was boiling with rage, seeing Daneesha at the school filled me with a small ounce of pride. I felt like a father who'd just successfully taught his only child how to ride a bike without training wheels.

We walked into the school together just seconds after the first warning bell. Daneesha gave me a quick hug and immediately sat down on the couch near the window to wait for her name to be called. My mind instantaneously went back to the obnoxious day ahead of me. I hoped and prayed that maybe I'd be able to arrive, sign in, and be on my way to start my final workday as a teacher without any issues. My prayers went unanswered.

"What are *you* doing here?" came Blanche's voice from behind me.

"Just here to enjoy my final day of employment, Mrs. Ellis," I responded politely.

"Don't you dare get all prim and proper with me, Mr. Cain. I expected you'd be hundreds of miles away by now with your tail tucked between your legs after the way you acted yesterday."

"Sorry to disappoint you."

"What in the hell do you think *you're* doing here?" came a menacing voice from my left as the door to the administrative offices swung open violently.

"Mrs. Raker, what an honor to get a greeting from you this morning, my final morning at this glorious institution," I said sarcastically.

I caught a quick glance in Daneesha's direction as she tried hard not to eavesdrop on what was going on. She appeared shocked at what I'd just said. I flashed a reassuring smile her way before turning back in the direction of the Devil in high heels.

"I'm honestly shocked that you had the gall to show up today after your colorful remark to me yesterday. And not to mention the lovely pictures of your apparent infidelity that wound up in everyone's mailboxes. I assumed you'd be halfway out of the country by now, seeing as your career and personal life are both likely over."

"With all due respect, Mrs. Raker, you've already flexed your muscles at me and demonstrated your power. And yes, my life is falling apart, thank you for noticing. But I doubt there's anything more you could say that would make things any worse than they already are."

"I beg to differ, Jackson," she said as she started to circle me like a shark from one side of my body to the other, "there's actually plenty of things I could say. For instance, how about the fact that, even though you're getting paid today, I've urged administration to consider getting a substitute for you? We've discussed it at length and we'd feel more comfortable with a sub handling your teaching duties instead of you. You've proven yourself rather inadequate time and time again."

"Fantastic," I said half-heartedly as I went to turn toward the exit, but she stopped me.

"Unfortunately, the only substitute we could get on such short notice can't make it in until sometime during fourth period. So we'd appreciate it if you'd get your ass up to your room and educate your students until the sub arrives."

I could feel the anger growing inside of me with every word this woman uttered. Every movement of her annoyingly smug demeanor just pissed me off. I wanted to wipe that condescending little smirk off of her ugly fucking face. But I couldn't do a damn thing. I could only smile painfully and walk toward my classroom in the farthest corner of the building one last time.

We all come with different degrees of sins. We all come with a backstory we're not particularly proud of. A backstory we've often tried to hide but as fate would have it always finds its way to the light. We all need to be exposed for our transgressions.

Gary the Head Custodian never should have shown me how to access the intercom on the building's phones. My finger hovered over the dial and twitched frantically in anticipation of accessing the intercom and putting on a public shit show. Maybe I should wait. Wait until the sub arrives and hide out in the break room until the end of the day, and then access the intercom. That's what I'll do. I'll wait it out and call an assembly in the auditorium.

My substitute arrived later than I thought he would. There couldn't have been any more than five minutes left during my lunch period when I received a knock on my door and a bald, overweight Haitian gentleman relieved me of my duties. I was rather happy that he didn't arrive during the first two periods. I didn't want to have to explain anything to the few students who would actually care about what was going on. I quietly grabbed my things, looked around my classroom and vaguely recalled the handful of memories and triumphs I wished to relive, before the incessant failures and hopeless students overwhelmed me to my core as I finally buried it all inside me and walked out my door for the final time.

The bell rang and the students crowded the hallways. It was third block. Everything was moving in slow motion. I felt like a ghost as everyone pushed through and around me. I watched the animals roam the hallways for nearly four minutes before it quieted down. It would have been my planning period right now. I could use a stiff drink. The endorphins in my body have been running rampant ever since I walked through the front of the building this morning. The storm was still brewing inside, growing stronger in intensity with every passing second. I was the eye of the storm, and I was ready to destroy everything in my path.

I passed by Perry's classroom on my way to the break room and peeked in his window. I could faintly hear him giving a brief end-of-the-year lecture as he walked around the room. It actually sounded like a heartfelt message on the importance of following your heart instead of your head, and doing whatever you believe in that heart of yours is right, despite what everyone else tells you. Follow *your* dreams, not others'. I had no idea that Perry could be that deep. Perhaps there was a passionate teacher hidden somewhere underneath his rugged, devil-may-care exterior.

Just as I started to walk away from Perry's door I heard a student ask him what he planned to do over his summer, "Gibbs, you's headin' back up north for the summer or are you's stayin' local?"

The question halted me in my tracks. It wasn't the question that set my mind on edge. The question was meaningless, for that matter. But did I hear that name correctly? Gibbs?

I slowly positioned my body back in front of Perry's door and examined his room. He'd already taken a lot of stuff down off the walls and packed them up, but his whiteboard still had some writing on it. Mostly comments and well wishes from students directed to him, and rather disturbingly a few phone numbers and Twitter handles jotted down for Perry to keep in contact with them. One comment in particular solidified my anger. There it was as plain as day on the man's whiteboard next to a pointless compliment of "You da' man": *Gibbs*. Janice had mentioned to me as she was kicking me out this morning that she had in fact cheated on me with a man named Gibbs who she said she'd met at Sex Addicts Anonymous.

Decorum and common sense had exited my body with a flourish. All that was left was impropriety and stupidity. I did the first thing I could think of and burst through Perry's door for the second time in less than a week.

"You low-life piece of shit!" I shouted as I wrapped my hands around Perry's collar and pinned him up against the wall.

His students were shocked and aimlessly moved near the back of the room out of the way of the ensuing altercation.

"Oh my, to what do I owe the pleasure of this greeting, Jack?" he chuckled thinking it was some sort of off-color joke.

I was enraged. I could feel my blood boiling underneath my skin. There were daggers in my eyes. I just wanted to gut Perry like a fish and watch his entrails pour out onto the floor.

"Don't you dare play stupid with me you son of a bitch! You know damn well what this is about you fucking prick!"

"Honestly, Jack, I really am in the dark here," he winced in fright as the pain behind my eyes and in my voice could clearly be felt by him as my uneasy tone escalated.

"What were you doing last night?" I asked, even though I already knew the answer would likely contain the image of Janice's waist being wrapped around his cock.

"I went to Sex…um," Perry started as he realized his students were still present in the room and that he should still attempt to exercise some caution with what he discusses in front of them, "that meeting you wanted me to look into when we had our little discussion the other day. And I was right, my friend. I met someone my age! I told you it would be a good place to meet chicks."

"Yeah, you did. By any chance did you happen to catch her name?"

"Of course I did! I believe it was Janice Simmons, or something like that. Why?"

My grip tightened around his throat as I shouted, "That's my girlfriend, pal. Well, ex-girlfriend *now.*"

I watched the life in Perry's eyes disappear. His expression went entirely pale as mine grew more and more red.

"Are you messing with me?"

"Does it look like I'm fucking messing with you, you dumb shit?" I shrieked.

"Um, class. You're dis–," he started to mumble.

"No," I interrupted, "no, stay right where you are. All of you!"

"Jack, what exactly is it that you plan on doing to me in the middle of my own classroom, in front of all my students? Let's just send them out into the hall and we can talk about this man to man, friend to friend."

"You're no friend of mine, *Gibbs.* You're nothing but scum. You're the lowest form of excrement there is. You're not going to work your magic on me today with your fucking charm and word bribery. You sleep with students half your age and you sleep with my girlfriend and you think we can just push it aside and act like nothing ever happened? Are you fucking stupid or just plain insane?"

The crowd of children gasped at the remark about Perry sleeping with students, which he tried to play off with a quick smirk and soft shake of his head, but my grip tightened even more and he grew still again.

"I'm positive that I have no idea what you're talking about, Jack," he mumbled with uncertainty.

"You can't possibly cover your tracks now, Perry. There are witnesses. In fact," I loosened my grip and pointed to a girl in the back of the room with a low cut shirt on, "it appears that at least one of them knows firsthand that they've had your cock in their mouth. Isn't that right, sweetie?"

The young girl shrunk down and hid her face into her hands, while the other students remained glued to the ground like statues.

"You're a fucking asshole," Perry snapped.

"Maybe I am, but you'll be the one rotting in Hell."

I reluctantly released him and turned as if I were about to walk away before quickly spinning around and connecting a giant blow to Perry's nose. He slammed backward against the wall and slumped defeated on the floor with blood gushing down his cheeks into a pool of crimson in his cupped hands.

"If I go down, I'm taking you with me," Perry muttered faintly as I inched closer to the door.

"I look forward to hearing that bullshit story. Enjoy the rest of your class, dick," I exclaimed as I rushed into the hallway in a calming fit of rage. The storm is gaining strength.

I guess I can see now how Colton was so upset with Jim all those years ago. Being cheated on by your girlfriend fucking sucks. Being cheated on by your girlfriend *with* someone who's supposed to be your best friend, sucks so much worse.

The National Weather Service has issued a severe shit storm warning for the following areas: North Grayson High School in Obella Falls, Florida. Stay indoors and seek immediate shelter.

The remaining minutes of third block continued to tick away in slow succession as the overwhelming urge to interrupt everyone's daily routines with an uncensored broadcast of the Jackson Cain Show was growing more and more intense.

I could use a stiff drink to calm my nerves. I began to wonder if Bill Starks happened to have anything left on him that I could salvage. Just a sip or two from his flask could truly do miracles for my infuriating mood. I walked passed his room just in case he happened to be in there attempting to be productive seeing as it was inching ever closer to the last block of the school year. There was absolutely no commotion inside as I gingerly strolled by his door and peeked through the window. The lights were off, shades were pulled, and boxes lined the floor near the front of the room. There was only one other place Bill could possibly be: the uncharted break room.

The English hallway appeared deserted. Posters were off the wall and papers were strewn along the floor. The only thing missing were tumbleweeds blowing in a western wind. It felt eerie as I crept along the isolated terrain toward the break room entrance at the end of the hallway.

I can't recall a time where this part of the building felt so strange and mysterious. Was the storm that was brewing inside me casting a dark shadow over every inch of the building I intended to destroy with my thunderous force? All life was evidently absent from this little nook situated in the corner of Hell. Maybe Bill wasn't over here after all.

I turned the key in the handle of the break room door and pushed it in. Nobody in the copier room. I poked my head inside each bathroom. Not a single soul. There must be someone in the lounge, at least. I nudged the door to the lounge only slightly and peered into its depths. Sure enough, an old familiar body was sitting on the divan at the edge of the room. Bill sat in his usual Al Bundy like pose, but this time was without his flask at his lips as his eyes were closed and his head tilted backward slightly.

An odd time of the day to be taking a nap, so close to last block, I thought.

Not wanting to disturb him just yet, I made my way over to the coffee machine and turned it on and thumbed through a magazine off the rack on the wall while the liquid brewed.

Every few seconds I glanced up at Bill to see if he'd woken up, but he remained slouched in his mid-afternoon slumber. He's been a teacher for nearly forty years in various school systems. If anybody had the knowledge of how drastically different education has become since he first started teaching in 1975, it would be him. He's taught through it all. The Cold War, the Persian Gulf War, the Yugoslav Wars, the War on Terror in Iraq and Afghanistan, and the War on Common Core. He's experienced the first frame *and* the second frame of that cartoon. Although he's undoubtedly lost a step or two here and there, that's quite an accomplishment for anyone to stick with one career for such a long time and put up with that much bullshit and that much change. He's got a thick skin despite it all and found a remedy that's pushed him through it for all these years: alcohol.

If I could become anyone, I'd probably choose him.

I glanced up at the clock and realized that the end of third block was waning down. Nearly fifteen minutes before the bell would ring and the whole school would be 80 minutes closer to summer vacation.

"Hey Bill, rise and shine! Don't you think you oughta be heading to your room? Planning period is almost over," I observed as I casually placed a lid over my coffee and took a small sip.

No response from Bill.

"Aloha, Earth to Bill! C'mon we gotta get going."

Still no response. Not even a glimmer of movement.

I moved briskly toward where Bill was sitting. His head was still tilted back, eyes closed, and a distinct odor of whiskey was emanating from his musk. His hands were displaced on either side of his waist with his flask adjacent to his right hand. There was a little bit of a stain on his polo shirt, most likely from the devil's liquid in his flask. This man must be dead drunk.

"Bill! Bill, you in there buddy?" I whispered as I lightly smacked him on each side of his face to encourage a response.

Nothing.

I sat down in the chair across from the divan wondering what I should do. There's no way that I could just leave him in here. He's likely got a class last block to teach. What will his students think if he doesn't show up? But at the same time, if I go and get somebody what will they do to him? Fire him? Force him to retire? It's not like he has a wife and a family to go home to. This little piece of Hell is all Bill has left.

But I needed to do something. If I leave him and he doesn't show up for last block, they're going to come looking for him. As I leaned forward to get out of the chair, out of the corner of my eye I noticed a black film canister laying horizontally on the floor with a few little white pills scattered about.

Immediately I began to panic as I crouched down to my knees. I couldn't quite figure out what kind of pills they were as none of them had any kind of engraving or marking on them. What were they doing all over the floor? Why did Bill have them to begin with? Why were they in an unlabeled film canister? What if…

Oh no. Not again.

I leaped to my feet wildly and lunged for Bill's body as I pressed my fingers against his neck hoping to find a pulse.

Nothing.

I was in shock. What am I supposed to do? I shook Bill violently and slapped him countless times across his face but there was no sign of life inside him. I quickly pushed his body down to the floor and started chest compressions and CPR. I could taste the whiskey on his breath as I gave him mouth to mouth, praying that he would breathe and that he and I would both wake up from this nightmare.

But there was nothing. No movement. No sound but my panicked whimpers and the ticking of the clock. Bill was gone.

"Why!?" I wailed as I back-pedaled away from Bill's lifeless body toward the base of the lounge door, "Why would you do something so stupid, Bill? Why!?"

No response. I was all alone.

"How could you!? Why?" I cried as tears streamed down my face, "You selfish son of a bitch, what in the hell were you thinking?"

In that moment, I wasn't sure if I was mad at Bill, or that just hours ago I was contemplating this exact scenario with myself, or if it were simply the fact that his lifeless body was lying in front of me and it was taking me back to Colton's death. Deep inside of me I could still feel a pulsating hatred for what Colton had done. Bill's lifeless body fed flashes of Colton's body on the concrete outside Jim's apartment. The image of Colton wouldn't leave my mind. It was hard enough the first time to lose my best friend. It wasn't any easier having to relive it.

The haunting echo of the clock ticking away each meaningless second of life grew painstakingly loud. Bill's dilapidated body lay motionless in front of me, just like mine lay motionless in front of his. I have had a lot of bad days as a teacher, but this was quite possibly one of the worst. It's one thing to deal with shitty students, annoying parents, and two-faced colleagues, but it's something entirely different to see a person you conversed with daily as cold as an icebox and stiff as a board on the floor of the teacher's lounge from an apparent suicide. Life can be pretty fucked up sometimes.

The clock continued its terrifying descent into the madness fourth block would entail. Only ten minutes separated me from revenge.

Nine. Eight. Seven.

Come on Father Time, speed it up.

Six. Five. Four.

I have so much to get off my chest.

Three. Two. One.

So many bridges to burn.

The bell sounded and reverberated persistently throughout the building. The time had come. It was finally here. *Show time.*

I wiped away the tears from my face and pressed the appropriate combination of buttons on the phone in the teacher's lounge to access the intercom. I heard the echo of the acoustics over the loudspeaker.

"Attention North Grayson High School, there is an emergency assembly being held in the auditorium. If you could please file into the hallway quietly and make your way there immediately, that would be greatly appreciated. Thank you," I stated calmly and efficiently as I hung up the receiver.

I picked up the receiver again and initiated a new sequence of numbers that would disable the intercom. Yet another nifty trick the crooked custodian taught me. I needed to disable it quickly for fear of administration attempting to access it and recant my assembly statement.

I rushed out of the teacher's lounge and sprinted down the hallway toward the auditorium. It was my time to shine. To unleash my fury on those who deserved to feel every ounce of my wrath. I likely wouldn't get much time so I needed to say my peace as quickly as possible, preferably before the police would inevitably arrive to escort me out of the building once and for all.

The auditorium was in a panicked uproar as no one knew what this sudden announcement was about. Administrators and security personnel were eagerly trying to rectify the situation and encourage everyone to head back to their rooms but hardly anyone was budging. I ran down the side of the auditorium toward the stairs and up to the stage. I knew exactly where the microphones were stashed offstage and picked one up and turned it on along with the sound system.

"Could I have everyone's attention please? Yes, look right up here at me. Thank you," I bellowed.

"What are you doing?" Mrs. Raker whispered angrily to me from the first row as her clenched fists shot at the ground.

"Not right now, bitch," I said to her out of earshot of the microphone as she rolled her eyes in disgust, "yes, everyone please find a seat and get comfortable. And when I have your attention I will begin."

The last remaining stragglers in the lobby filed into the auditorium and filled in the empty seats near the back. It was a full house. Students, teachers, custodians, administrators, and support staff. Everyone had arrived.

"I'm not sure if everyone is aware of this, but as of right now I am no longer an employee here at North Grayson High School. Feel free to let the shock of that news hit you on your own time, as I likely only have a few minutes to spare here. That news alone is not why I called this little assembly here today. I've called this assembly because I've got a few things I'd like to say to all of you. I've got shit I'd like to get off my chest, if you don't mind. I was let go as a teacher here because quite frankly, I didn't kiss enough ass. Perhaps if I were more like Blanche Ellis, maybe I would have been asked back next year regardless of how effective I am in the classroom. Maybe if I had kissed one more ass a week, I'd still be employed here like you my dear. Keep up the good work. You deserve it. I mean, your lips have puckered up quite a bit.

"But not nearly as much as the narcissistic Ms. Meadows. Speaking of puckered lips, Ms. Meadows gets around ladies and gentleman. Not only did she have a small part in ending my relationship with my girlfriend by misleading me into joining her for a bite to eat and instead seeing her at her second job as a stripper at Peeper's, but now everyone knows she's a stripper at Peeper's and yes, she delivers *happy endings* at this job. Which, last I checked, prostitution isn't what I would call legal in our state. Not to mention the plausibility of my being drugged by you. I do recall that that was the oddest tasting vodka I'd ever been force-fed. Thanks for helping me find out the ugly truth about many of the women in this area, Ms. Meadows. If you show even the least bit of attention to them, they'll drug you and fuck up your life if you attempt in any way to thwart their advances.

"And speaking of fucking up your life. Mrs. Raker, my mentor of the last three years, give her a hand ladies and gentleman. Or a certain finger, if you prefer. Nobody, and I mean nobody has the knack for being an unrelenting, self-absorbed, overwhelming bitch like Mrs. Raker. The woman who single-handedly saw to it that my tenure as a teacher would be destroyed. This she-devil spent the last three years making my life a living Hell. Nothing was ever good enough. And those of you who have had her as a teacher, know that that's the truth. Newsflash missy: you're not good enough either. Hence why you're still in the position you're in and not a true administrator. I swear I used to worry so much about seeing this woman's shadow in my vicinity, that I'd have nightmares about it. But not anymore. I leave her unto all of you poor individuals who have to continue to deal with her sneaky bullshit from here on out.

"But wait there's more. Don't get me started on sneaky bullshit. There's a couple of interesting factoids I just recently learned this week. This school has a few crafty teachers keeping secrets from everybody. Anyone know where I can purchase some good blasters up in this bitch? Oh, just see Demarcus Mitchell or Alberto Gonsalves you say? But they're not who we really want, are they? They're just pawns behind the Kingpin's master scheme. Is Clark Wellers in the house? There he is! I see you slouching down back there in the green shirt! C'mon stand up and take a bow you sneaky bastard. If you have any questions about any drugs you'd like to purchase to get a little high, just ask him. He can answer them all.

"What if that's not your forte? Maybe drugs aren't what you're about. Well say no more. Perhaps a little fornication to feed your sexual desires is more up your alley. We have yet another expert in our midst. He's got a little black book the size of his penis. Or so I've been told. I've never actually seen his penis. But a few of his students have. In fact, here's a funny story, you're just going to die. I mistakenly walked in on one of those said students blowing him like a trombone right at his desk during lunch. I was shocked to say the least. But he assured me, it wasn't a big deal and that he's been doing it for years and will likely continue to do it until he retires. Oh, and he's also the other component that lead to the destruction of my relationship with my girlfriend, my horny pal and former best friend, Mr. Perry Gibson. We've already talked today. You're quite welcome for that new nose job, buddy.

"Yes folks, it's a sad reality that so many staff members at this fine institution lead sick, twisted lives. And then there are others you think lead wonderful lives, but find out that they don't. Just this afternoon I went to the teacher's lounge in the English hallway after having been relieved of my duties by a substitute. And in that lounge do any of you know what I saw? Let's ask the students of Bill Starks. Did you happen to see your teacher as you made your way to his room this period? No, no you didn't. That's because the unfortunate drunk was in the teacher's lounge, sitting motionless on the divan, having committed suicide to escape his shitty life. The friendliest man in this building at face value, was probably the saddest of us all. I tried to revive him, but it was too late. I had considered drinking myself into an oblivion after the way things have transpired and progressively gotten worse each day this week. I wanted to become like him and suppress my problems with alcohol, much like he was doing every day. Because it seemed to be working. It looked like a manageable solution. But after seeing him like that, I can't do that to myself. This job, this place, these people here, it's not worth it. You're not worth it.

"And with that, I bid you farewell. I will not miss any of you. Fuck you all!" I shrieked loudly as I dropped the mic and proceeded to dish out the middle finger to the entire room. I jumped down off the auditorium stage and bolted toward the exits.

Much to my surprise the students all hopped up and applauded my elaborate speech and cheered for me as I made my escape. Students I had never met before, others I had never even seen, high-fived me as I scurried by them. I was free. I finally felt like a leaf caught in the wind. I felt weightless as I plowed through the front doors as mounds of students followed me into the parking lot hooting and hollering in elation.

I got to my Camaro and completely ransacked the trunk for a baseball bat. I swiftly cut between a couple cars to Perry's Corvette. Thankfully he had parked close to me today. Before I could even talk myself out of it, I started wailing away on every beautiful inch of his beloved vehicle. The cheers and yells of excitement still coming from the crowd of people behind me added fuel to my already burning adrenaline.

Perry rushed out of the building to see the commotion and stopped suddenly in his tracks, clearly uninterested to do battle with a man with a deadly weapon. I got to see him wince in utter agony with every menacing cut I took at his windshield, his headlights, the doors, and the hood, adding insult to injury from soup to nuts on his Corvette's frame. I swung with a vengeance until the powerful block of lumber between my hands could take no more and snapped in half.

Just as I dropped the shattered handle of what remained of my baseball bat my phone rang in my pocket. I quickly pulled it out and answered it, turning toward the crowd and pointing the jagged end toward Perry to keep him at bay.

"Hello, Jackson Cain speaking," I said.

"Jackson, it's Larry Helmer from the Helmer Balman Literary Agency. How are you doing today?" he asked.

My emotions were doing all sorts of twists and turns inside of me, "I'm having a day filled with a mix of emotions. But right now, I'm surprisingly calm. How are you doing sir?"

"I'm doing wonderful. Listen, I've read your novel manuscript and I was absolutely floored by it. There's no doubt about it I want to represent you and your work and I wanted to contact you firsthand to offer you representation. Are you interested?"

I was speechless. I didn't know what to say. My body was overcome with an immense satisfaction and joy that I wanted to just drop the phone and do cartwheels all over the parking lot.

"Hello, Jackson are you there?"

"Yes, yes I'm still here," I started, "I'm just overcome with incredible gratitude at the moment."

"Good, that's what I like to hear. So do we have a deal? Would you like to be a client of the Helmer Balman Literary Agency?"

"Absolutely," I confirmed.

"Excellent. I will finish fleshing out all of the paperwork and give you a call back later today to solidify the details and we will get into business of searching for the perfect publisher for you. I hope you're ready my friend, your life is definitely about to change for the better."

And with that last remark Larry hung up and I brought down the phone from my ear. After a moment I threw my arms up in the air, flashed a huge smile, and glared with an immense relief up to the heavens. The sun broke through the clouds and shined its light brightly down on me. It was as if in that single moment I were the only one there. My prayers had been answered. I'd suffered enough. Things had finally begun to come together.

With one last fleeting glare at the flock of people crowding the front entrance, I dived into my Camaro and sped off into the distance, tossing a special finger out the driver's side window.

The wind on my arm felt soothing. The sunshine on my face felt calming. I was finally free. Free to live my life and do whatever. The weight had been lifted. I was on a mission to find Happiness. A place that exists in your mind that is only reachable through dreams.

The path to Happiness is scattered with obstacles meant to slow you down. If you don't rise up to the challenge and try to push through, you will always remain in limbo. Your road signs will always be unclear and you'll always drive in circles.

I guess it's true what they say, life is tough, and in order to survive it, you've got to be tougher. If you surround yourself with the right people, *good people*, people who don't make your life tougher than it already is, it won't seem quite as bad. I haven't surrounded myself with the right people in a long time. It's about time I do. I'm long overdue for a bit of Happiness.

I have no time to dwell on the images in my rearview mirror, as the road in front of me is what carries my future. I *was* a teacher. Now I'm moving on to something else, something better. I haven't the slightest clue just yet where I'll end up, but I do know one thing…I'm *never* going back to where I was.

I picked up my phone and dialed a number I used to instinctively dial all the time when I was younger, but one that I hadn't dialed in a few years. I half-hoped to be greeted by Colton's warm voice ready to jokingly berate me for not having called him in a long time, but I knew that wouldn't happen. But the calm of knowing everything was suddenly different soothed me in putting that slim slice of hope that we'd entered an alternate universe where everything that used to be was back to normal.

"You've reached Colton," began the automated voicemail message, "you know what to do."

At the sound of the beep, I simply smiled and said, "I'm heading toward the horizon, buddy. I'm no longer going nowhere. I'm going *everywhere.*"

I ended the call and glanced down at my passenger's seat and saw the empty journal Carter had left me at the bar soaking up the sun. With a quick movement, I turned to the first page as I careened aimlessly down the road. The first part of the message was smudged and hardly visible, but even still the remaining message spoke to me loud and clear.

Keep moving toward the horizon. Write your future, it's in your hands. It's always been in your hands.

As my eyes went back and forth between road and journal, I saw a new line scribbled at the bottom of the page. And I knew then that I was going to be all right. I knew then that I was on the right path, that all of the shit that I'd been through over the years was just debris thrown in my way in attempt to divert my path. But I kept trudging through, just like I was supposed to. Carter Corrish, whether he was real or simply a manifestation of everything I hoped to be I will never know, had found a way to speak to me once more. He knew exactly where I was headed.

Happiness – *Next Exit.*

I guess I've been within driving distance of Happiness all along. I guess I just needed that little push to go searching for it. I needed to let go of the hands that I thought were guiding me to where I wanted to be, but were instead holding back. It feels good to finally be free.

I glanced out the passenger's side window and noticed that I wasn't the only one gliding along the pavement toward the horizon. A single robin moving at the exact pace of my car joined me. I smiled at the fleeting thought of my recurring dream over the years. I'd finally caught up with the robin. He was no longer miles ahead of me and out of reach. We were together. We were going to the same place.

I need to make things right with those I care about and take them along for the ride of my life.

I'm not sure if Darlene and little Carter, Jr. will still be at Pinewood Suites, but with this newfound confidence instilled inside of me, I'm determined to find them if they aren't and make up for years of lost time.

I never knew what Happiness was, until I stopped stressing over finding it. I guess, in a way, I'm just like Chief Bromden.

I've been away a long time.

www.ingramcontent.com/pod-product-compliance
Lightning Source LLC
Chambersburg PA
CBHW020617180626
46810CB00007B/2820